A STAR FOR
THE LATECOMER

Brooke Hillary is an attractive, sixteen-year-old girl
whose mother, Claire, is ambitious for her daughter to
become the star dancer she herself always wanted to be.
Brooke loves her mother dearly, and does her best to
make her dreams come true by working hard at the
special school for talented young artists she attends in
Manhattan. But secretly Brooke has her own dreams –
of falling passionately in love with a fabulous boy and
having three kids of her own. To her, love comes first
and success in dancing second.

Then, tragically, Brooke learns that her mother is
fatally ill. It becomes a race against time to make a
success of her dancing while her mother can still enjoy
it, and Brooke's first love affair looks certain to be
nipped in the bud.

'A beautifully crafted piece of fiction. The language and
plot are fast and lean, and yet carry a story that reaches
into our quieter, thinking parts.'   *Reading Time*

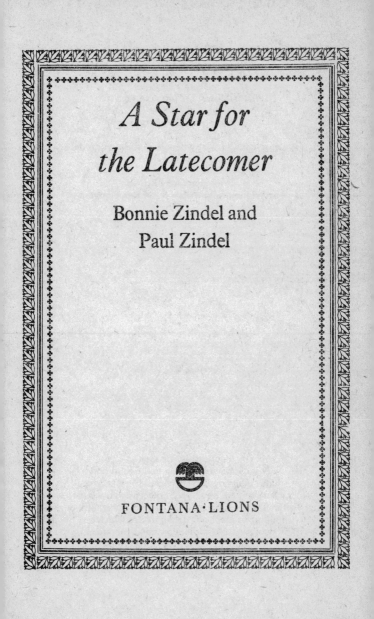

A Star for the Latecomer

Bonnie Zindel and
Paul Zindel

FONTANA·LIONS

First published in USA 1980 by Harper & Row, Inc.,
New York
First published in Great Britain 1980 by
The Bodley Head Ltd
First published in Fontana Lions 1981
by William Collins Sons & Co Ltd
14 St James's Place, London sw1

Printed in Great Britain
by William Collins Sons & Co Ltd, Glasgow

To
loving parents
Claire and Jack

1

I'm seventeen years old now and it's been a year since what happened happened. I can't keep it inside me any longer, and although I've never met you, I feel somehow you'll understand because you're probably around my age or once upon a time you were my age.

I've got to tell my story to someone because my heart will break if I don't, and the story I'm going to tell you is about a girl—me—who wanted to go for ice cream sodas at Rudley's after school with friends and dream about falling in love with a boy who would keep staring at me from across the room as he sipped his root beer float and we'd wind up having root beer floats happily ever after.

I went to school every day just like you might do now, but I went to a peculiar school. It was different from the public schools most kids go to. This was a special school for kids who were supposed to become stars of one sort or another; and *stars* could mean anything from singers to dancers to clowns to magicians. My school was a haven for young people filled with high hopes and exalted dreams, some more realistic than others, and others more realized. One interesting thing about my school, besides having an elevator which we were permitted to ride, was we had telephones in every classroom in case someone was trying to reach one of us for an important audition. Some were seriously studying music or dance or acting, and many were working professionally. That phone was our link with possible work during the school day.

I liked dancing, but I didn't like performing in front of people. Since I'm somewhat shy, the thought of an audience staring at me made me sick with fright. The pre-performance jitters outweighed the joy I got from dancing itself. But more than liking to dance, I liked making my mother happy, and I knew that my dancing made her very, very happy. And since I wanted her approval and love, I thought it best to keep on dancing. This can put great pressure on a kid.

Some days I didn't feel like taking a gymnastics class. What I really felt like doing was taking a casual walk around Green Acres Shopping Center with a friend, trying on skirts, or simply going home, washing my hair and daydreaming.

Some of the kids at school really wanted to practice the piano four hours a day or be whirling on the ice at five in the morning. They never complained. They were the ones who were good at what they did because they loved what they were doing and I admired them. Then, there was me.

At my school we were supposed to be getting an education like most kids, though it was quite a trick to keep our minds on schoolwork. You never knew when that phone would ring and someone would call to ask you to come down for a soap commercial—or maybe a movie producer would come through algebra class looking for a new kid to star in his next movie.

We had no basketball team or football field or anything like that at our school, which was in the middle of Manhattan; all we had was a Ping-Pong table. We not only had ice skaters, actors, cellists, concert pianists, rock singers—we even had kids from famous parents. One boy, for example, was the son of America's finest stripper, who became famous for what she did best and they even wrote a Broadway musical about her. Then there was *me*. I was a kid who wasn't famous and didn't come from famous parents. It was just plain me—Brooke Hillary—who lived on Long Island and had to commute one hour each way to a unique school which gave a student great leeway in pursuing a career while studying. Many kids would be away from school for months at a time making movies or trying out shows before bringing them to Broadway, and they wouldn't miss a day's work because all our reading assignments in each class were carefully mapped out on a correspondence sheet for each semester. A student would simply follow the assignment sheet and mail in the homework each week. I never had to mail in anything because I never left.

My parents wanted me to be a dancer. It was their dream from the time I was three years old and the doctor said my left leg needed a little strengthening and that dancing might help. My mother saw this as a great opportunity to make me into something special. She wanted to give me opportunities she had missed while growing up. The problem was that being a mother and wife was not enough for her and she liked to fantasize about what we'd do one day when we went out to Hollywood.

I remember in the sixth grade I hated Wednesday afternoons, when my mother picked me up early from school to take me to a dance class in Manhattan, and the children would all whisper about me as I left the room. I didn't want the kids whispering about me. I didn't want to be different, but I didn't tell my mother. There were always a few dancers in my class who *were* exceptional, and there were always some girls prettier than me, with better figures; but to my mother, sitting there with other mothers, looking radiant, I was a wonder. In my mother's eyes I was tops. When I knew she was watching, I tried to have more elevation in my jumps, lift my leg higher, because in her eyes I could jump ten feet off the ground and I didn't want to spoil her illusion.

"After all, you stand as good a chance as any," my mother said early on in the lessons. She wasn't any great choreographer or dance expert or anything like that. My mother was just a simple housewife in Elmont, best known for bacon, lettuce and tomato sandwiches.

But if she wanted me to be a great dancer, it was good enough for me. My mother was one of the smartest people I ever met, and I say that without prejudice. She could read a book with such concentration that I could walk into the room and she wouldn't even know I was there, until I tickled her toes or something. We used to laugh at how involved she got in her novels.

She could handle any situation. When I asked her how she got smart she'd answer, "Experience." And that was one thing I didn't have and desperately wanted.

I had dreams of falling in love with a fabulous boy and having three kids who I would take to the park. We'd roll down the steep hills together, getting covered with leaves and grass, and look like a salad. Then we'd go home to my husband, who would love me just the way I was, leaves and all. With all that, I could have a career too, but love came first. To my mother, though, love came second. She wanted me to be a success before anything. She said this was the time in my life for me to develop myself, and to be a little selfish, and being selfish wasn't a bad word, it just had a bad reputation because it meant that you liked yourself enough to want to do what was best for yourself. Once she said, "If you're selfish with goodness, you can't be stopped."

My life must have seemed exciting to other kids on my block, yet there were parts of their lives that I envied. I wanted to know a boy in the neighborhood who would walk me home after school and share things with me, who would put his arm around me, and love me, and bring me flowers, and care when I was sick. Someone to share the journey of growing up.

Some kids in our neighborhood had coupled off, and their closeness seemed special. I wanted someone to be close to, someone who would travel with me into awkward places, places I had never been before, like trusting, experimenting, confiding and sharing secrets with each other the way my parents did. Maybe that's what my mother called "experience." I wanted to have a boy put his arm around me, and for me not to feel frightened. I wanted to be in love because I had so much love building up in me and needed someone to share it with. I didn't want puppy love, or calf's love, or platonic love. I yearned for the real thing, whatever it is. If love is simple and universal, why is it one of the hardest things to find?

There was one boy with blond curly hair whom I particularly liked. His name was Brandon and he was a little older than most of us. He seemed a very nice person who was just himself. He was a perfect combination of the boy next door and the boy of your dreams. His mouth curled up at the bottom into a contagious smile and his eyes had a glimmer that made me feel his mind was always working. It made me have to work to keep my mind working, too. He was very natural and refreshing compared to the rest of the kids. I think that's what attracted me to him so much. And this attraction to Brandon was the first feeling I remember from last year—the "Terrible Year," as it turned out to be.

The unhappiness started, I suppose, when I was coming home from school one day last September. A boy at the Elmont train station yelled out to me, "Hey,

Ruby Lips, how was the freak show today? Hey, Snow White, I'm talking to you!" He had this ghastly sadistic smile and I just kept walking toward my house. But it's funny how *mean* kids have an ability to put a zing on the truth. He made me begin to wonder if I was a freak and didn't even know it. Maybe I did wear too much makeup. Maybe my hair was too severe, not long the way most girls were wearing it. And sometimes I would wear a silly hat to school because my mother thought it looked interesting. Maybe I was freakish instead of interesting.

So much depends on what world you live in. I wasn't doing what the other kids on the block were doing, but the rest of the kids on my block weren't doing what the kids in my school were doing either. I don't know what that boy who called me Ruby Lips would have thought of Nancy, my best girl friend from school, who had to go four times a week to be stretched and had hair three feet long. Her father insisted Nancy go to this special clinic where they put her on a machine that stretched her body because he felt she would have to be at least five feet four to be seriously considered as a skater.

So I walked down the street feeling miserable. The leaves were falling and there was a strange sadness in the air. I kept walking toward our six-room house, where I lived with my mother, father and brother Pete. Pete is three years older than me, which made him nineteen. He didn't know where he was going, which didn't upset him though it did upset my parents. One evening he had had too many beers at the local pizza palace and put his fist through a glass door. My parents asked him why he didn't just turn the doorknob like everyone else, but Pete said it was just that kind of night when everything went wrong. Pete was nice, but a few strong drinks changed him from a peaceful person into a steamroller. To some people it looked like Pete got shortchanged in the family, that I got all the attention, special classes and special schools. But Pete knew exactly what he was doing. He was smart and silent and saw everything and said very little. He kept his thoughts and feelings to himself usually, but sometimes he allowed me to see them by his grimaces, for instance when my father asked why he didn't shut off the lights in his room when he went out. Pete's eyes would dart over to me telling me his entire feelings in a fraction of a second, but he would not answer my father. He didn't want anyone to control his life. That's one particular point where Pete and I were totally different. Pete didn't go to Aunt Faye's with us if he didn't feel like it because he didn't need to please my mother or Aunt Faye. He simply did what he wanted. As for myself, even when I knew what my own desires were, my parents' love was more important to me.

Pete never seemed to have an inner struggle—his manner was peaceful, his body strong. I admired Pete's independence. If only I could be more like him and try pleasing myself instead of my parents. What if I had been an orphan and had the freedom to pick whatever I wanted to be, would I really want to dance on my own? When the house was empty, I would turn on the stereo and dance and pour my heart out to an imaginary figure. It was then that I danced best—as well as anyone in my class—but as soon as anyone was watching I'd clam up. I couldn't express private feelings in public.

The day after that creep called me "Ruby Lips" was Friday the thirteenth. I had nothing against the number, but I hated Fridays because they meant spending the weekend alone and not seeing my friends for two days, especially Brandon and Nancy. Sometimes I wondered how I would get through the weekend. As soon as I came home from school on Friday I used to begin the countdown until Monday morning by busying myself with homework, jogging, sleeping and eating and talking on the telephone. Monday finally arrived. I knew it when I heard "Good morning. Time to get up" from the foot of the stairs. How could my mother be so happy at seven in the morning?

"Brooke? Brooke? Are you up?" Her voice becoming more forceful, but today I sensed it missing her usual perky ring.

"I'm up," I yelled downstairs, jumping out of bed and opening my white shutters, infusing my room with bright sunlight that warmed my skin. I stood there a minute basking in it, thinking, *How wonderful it's finally Monday and in a few hours I'll be in school again.* Then I threw some water on my face to wake up my mind. I patted the water on my face with all ten fingers, pinching my cheeks a little to increase the circulation, a beauty tip I read in a glamor magazine. Then I put some makeup on and mascara, and I noticed my expression changing as I put on my "face." I felt I was hiding behind something, but it seemed safe. Then I remembered the boy who'd called after me. Most of the girls at school wore makeup, and I wondered if they still felt as insecure as I did. Was that kid right?

I threw on my purple skirt and Indian blouse and almost fell down the fifteen steps following the smell of percolating coffee. My brother was still sleeping and my father had already left for work. My mother buttered my English muffin just the way I like it, letting the butter get into all the little crevices so that it oozed out when I bit it. She pulled the belt of her flannel bathrobe tighter and sat down with what must have been her sixth cup of coffee for the morning. "Mom, why do you drink so much coffee?" I asked. "Have your milk," she said, smiling. By now I was waking up and becoming conscious as I looked into her face, noticing as I always did her large blue eyes. I also noticed her eyes looked a little sad, and I saw wrinkles around her lids that I had never noticed before. There was a look about her that scared me. I hated to think that my mother was getting older. I wanted her to stay eternally thirty and eternally unchanged. We both enjoyed the changes taking place in me, but time was my friend. It allowed me to grow up; time was my mother's enemy because it made her grow old too quickly. The last six months had been difficult for her. She had been to the hospital several times for tests and she didn't have the energy she used to.

"What's the matter, Mom?" I would ask her when she would need to rest after running up the stairs.

"Just a temporary slowdown, honey. Some people call it change of life, but as you see I haven't changed," she'd say.

"People don't go to the hospital for a change of life," I said. "Please tell me why you go."

"I've been getting tired and the doctors think it's a chemical imbalance. I'll be okay," she said. Obviously to change the subject, she walked over to her pocketbook, which was sitting on the kitchen counter next to the toaster, and pulled out a check.

"Brooke, this is for this month's dance classes at the Ballet Arts. I know this term is going to bring you luck. I can almost taste it, that's how confident I am. Call it intuition."

"I hope so." I smiled, still wondering about her.

"I can see it now. *Starring Brooke Hillary!*" she said as she moved her hand slowly as if reading a marquee. She seemed to be actually reading the letters in front of her. I went over to take the check and give her a big hug.

"What are you going to do today?" I asked. She sipped her coffee, then looked at me. "I'll run around the house with the vacuum cleaner, then Dad wants me to pick up some pajamas for him from the store." Her eyes moved quickly away from mine and we both felt there was some strange intimacy about the word pajamas that was not suitable for breakfast talk. I thought how great it was that she and my father were so close. I envied her that.

"Mom," I asked, "do you think a person can live without being loved?"

"Brooke"—my mother looked back at me—"what made you ask that?"

"I was just thinking." I stirred my chocolate milk and licked the spoon clean. "I was just thinking: That couple across the street—he always walks to the train four feet in front of his wife every morning, like ducks in a lineup. I'd rather die than live like that," I said.

"Some people learn to live with very little love," she said.

"Not me," I said defiantly. "I want a whole lot of it." Then I drank my milk. "Mom," I asked, remembering that kid who'd called me Ruby Lips, "do you think anyone will ever love me?"

"More than you'll be able to handle," my mother said, smiling. "Be patient. When the time is right, everything will come to you." She got up and put a piece of bread into the toaster. "Honey, you're only sixteen. It wasn't until I was twenty-two and I was with my girl friends at Brighton Beach in Brooklyn that someone hit me over the head with a baseball bat. That's how I met your father. He knocked me out. When I came to I was lying on the sand with a man standing over me patting me frantically. In my whole life I never saw anyone so excited that my eyes were open. His big green eyes were staring right into mine and he was smiling. His nose was slightly curved to the left, but he had a kind face. He asked if he could take me home and I told him I lived in the Bronx, but he said it didn't matter, he *wanted* to."

"Now *that's* romantic," I pointed out.

"I suppose it was." My mother smiled, her eyes drifting as though she were literally going back in time. "We had to take the IND subway. We just jabbered away and laughed, and by the time we reached the Bronx I knew I would never be lonely again. If love can bloom underground on the IND somewhere between Brooklyn and the Bronx, it can happen anywhere."

My mother was so easy to love. She exuded enthusiasm and she made everything and everyone feel alive. Anything in the world was possible, according to my mother, if you wanted it badly enough and worked for it. She always stood up for me. Once she went to school to speak to the teacher when I was stuck with a C in English because of a computer foul-up. All my friends loved her; they adopted her as their mother away from home. One friend called her "Mama Hillary." And they loved sitting around the white Formica kitchen table having talks with her as a confidante. They'd ask her advice on boyfriends and she'd be so wise. When my girl friend Joy's parents went away for three weeks in the summer my mother said she could stay with us. Those were terrific weeks during the summer when we didn't get dressed until three in the afternoon. My mother brought us breakfast in bed and let us just be lazy, play games, talk, play cards. We weren't expected to do anything except clean up after dinner. I swept the floor and Joy cleared the table. When Mom'd be running around the house with the vacuum cleaner and we'd feel a little guilty and offer to help, she'd say, "Now you two just enjoy yourselves. You're only young once," as if she knew something about getting older we didn't know.

She made me want to do anything in the world to make her happy. I wanted her approval on everything. I would say, "Mother, do you like this one?" when we'd go out shopping for a dress, or "Mother, do you like these shoes or should I buy the others?" In my dance classes, sometimes I'd be doing exercises and I'd see her reflection in the mirror even though she wasn't in the room. Sometimes I'd be spinning and spinning around, doing turns, and wouldn't know where she began and I ended. We were like the forest and the trees, one couldn't exist without the other. I loved her more than anyone on earth and I knew she loved me more than my father and brother. I didn't realize that that put a very heavy responsibility on me for her happiness. I'm sure she didn't either.

"Mom?" I asked, finishing my glass of chocolate milk. "Sometimes I think you're the only one who will really love me."

She came around the table and gave me a big hug, and as she did a piece of her hair, usually combed off her face, fell onto my cheek and tickled me, and I knew exactly which hairs. It was the few strands of gray running through, the ones she had given me a penny a hair to pull out last summer. Now twice as many gray hairs grew back and I could feel the stiffer texture as I giggled to myself, wanting to see how long I could stand being tickled without screaming out. I remembered back to all the times I asked my mother to tickle me just so I could feel that fine line between pleasure and pain. She knew my weak points along my back that no one else had discovered yet, and had been tickling me there for years.

"How did you get so insecure?" she said supportively.

"I guess I have been ever since I was little," I said, lightly trying to cover up my vulnerability.

"You must believe in yourself, but you must feel it in *here*," she said pointing toward her heart. "Inside yourself!

"People look for Mars and Jupiter in the skies, but inside of us is where we find our own dreams. And if I'm ever not around to keep reminding you, you must always believe you're something special. Do you understand me, Brooke? Dear, you must remember!"

She seemed to be staring right through me as though she knew how different I felt inside, but all I could hear was *If I'm ever not around to keep reminding you. If I'm ever not around.* What did she mean by that—"not around"? Not around? Where was she going that she wouldn't be around? Then I felt an anxiety attack coming on, the kind that feels like a balloon blowing up inside my chest and pressing against my heart, like I'm suffocating. The balloon feels very big inside me, and I feel very small. I think that's what they call an anxiety attack.

"What do you mean—'not around'?" I managed to get the words out, watching her face for every nuance of expression, looking for hidden meanings.

"Brooke, you can't expect me to always be there

to give you confidence; it's time you started believing in yourself," she said firmly. There was a certain coldness in her voice; no, it was more like she was removing herself from what she was saying, and it frightened me.

Desertion. That's what I was feeling. It sounded like she was deserting me and I wanted her to stay always, wanted to know she would always be my loyal partner.

2

The Long Island Railroad was my roller coaster to school every day. I called it that because no matter how many times I rode it I never knew what turn was coming up ahead. Just when I'd think I knew where the next curve was, there was a surprise. Even though it meant leaving my neighborhood behind, a ride from Elmont, where my folks had moved to give my brother and me a better life, to Manhattan, where my mother wanted me to go to school, was exhilarating to me. The train would speed along and sometimes I'd spend the time dreaming about my life instead of doing my homework.

Toward the end of September, I was on the train heading to school and I had a terrible sense of foreboding. My mother had been chewing her food the night before when she'd cried out in pain and started to cry.

"It's just a tooth," she said quickly when she saw me looking at her.

"Is there anything I can do?" I said, starting to get up.

"No," Mom said, reassuringly. "Just finish eating."

But something *was* wrong. My mother had been going to the hospital more often, and quite an arsenal of pills was building up in the medicine cabinet. She tried convincing me she was working on body chemistry.

"Why do you take Mother to the clinic so much?" I tried asking my father.

"The doctor just checks her blood," he said.

"What for?" I pursued, feeling anxious and full of fear.

"She needs vitamins, that's all," he said.

But I knew something else was happening.

So this morning my mother didn't mention the pain or her crying, and I didn't bring up the topic over breakfast because if she was in pain, and trying to concentrate on something else to take her mind off it, I didn't want to remind her. But I kept thinking of it on the train.

We pulled into Pennsylvania Station and I dashed to catch the Seventh Avenue local to Columbus Circle. I rushed up the stairs and Nancy was waiting for me, her chestnut hair reaching down to her waist. We always met so that we could walk the three blocks to school together.

"Hi," I said.

"Hi," Nancy said.

I was out of breath. "Have you been waiting long?" I asked.

"Nope. I just got here." Nancy smiled as we fell into stride. "Guess what?" she offered. "*Brandon* called. Did he call you, too?" she asked.

"Nope," I said disappointedly.

"Well, his father yelled that he should get off the phone because he was on too long with me, so that's probably why he didn't get to you," she said sympathetically.

There was something lovely and special about Nancy. She always knew what I was feeling and she treated my feelings with great gentleness. I tried doing the same thing with her.

"I just think Brandon doesn't like me," I confessed.

"Maybe he didn't call you because he *does* like you," Nancy suggested.

"What do you mean?"

"It's easy for him to call me because we're just friends. Maybe you're more than a friend to him and that's why he can't call you."

That reverse logic made perfect sense and I wanted to believe it.

"Oh no, no," I said anyway. "I'm sure that's not it. He probably can't stand me," I added, taking my usual defeatist attitude about myself ever having a real friendship with a boy. But deep inside I wished there was one iota of truth in what Nancy said. I liked Brandon too much. I always managed to like boys who hardly noticed me. There's one of the things I'd love to know about boys—if they do the *same* thing. Do they always pick out girls who hardly notice them? My mother said I did it on purpose. She said, "Why don't you pick out a boy who talks to you? That's important in beginning a friendship." She had a point there. Like in junior high school, I had a crush on a boy named Steve Mellrick who never once talked to me for the entire year. It's not that he didn't like me—he didn't even know me. We were in different classes, we'd never been introduced or bumped into each other by accident in the playground, but I got dressed every day for him. I fixed my hair extra special hoping he would notice me. I'm not complaining. I'm not saying that boys never liked me; it's just that the ones I liked never liked me back. Once a jockey picked me up for a blind date and fell in love with me. You should have seen the look on my mother's face when we opened the front door and there I was looking up to see my date and I had to look down about four inches. I think he liked me because I lived close to Belmont Race Track and was only five feet two. He was a very nice person and had interesting horse stories to tell. But I wasn't attracted to him.

And another problem I had was that I always liked my brother's friends who were three years older at least, and they had things on their minds that were always three years older than what my mother thought I should have on my mind. Most of the time when Pete's friends came over they'd march up to his room and he'd ask me to leave and close the door.

I wanted to sit outside just one time and listen to what older boys talk about but I knew they would've killed me if I'd been discovered. Sometimes I wondered if he was closing his friends out from me or me out from his friends, because Pete was a very protective brother. His cutest friend, Michael, would always stare at me as he walked past my bedroom, and he never left without saying, "Good-bye, Brooke," giving me a great big grin. I'd smile back, hoping once he'd stay and talk to me in my room for a few minutes. Michael's life seemed simple and unadorned, his face shone and I always wanted to reach out and touch the skin on his face. What would it be like if he picked me up for pizza instead of my brother and took me around the corner for a soda, and kissed me in front of the garage door while everyone was asleep, and brought me twelve American beauty roses for my birthday? What would it be like to be his girl, and wear his blue varsity jacket when the night air turned cool—and have him drop by each day because he missed me?

But Brandon was the same age as I was, and maybe if Nancy was right, there was hope.

Nancy opened the front door of the school and we went into the hallway. Miss Prendergast was at the front desk smiling at us as we signed in.

"Good morning, Nancy. Good morning, Brooke," she said.

"Good morning, Miss Prendergast," we said in unison.

At this point, Nancy and I had to part. I went to my first period, which was mythology with Mrs. Laven.

"How is mythology relevant to our lives today?" an aunt had asked me.

"It isn't," I'd replied, and that was just the reason why I liked it. I could fantasize about heros who had never existed.

Mrs. Laven was teaching this course as excitingly as if she had been reigning on Mount Olympus herself. She was my favorite teacher, because she made me feel as though what I had to say meant something, as though my opinion mattered, and I always tried hard to live up to her expectations of me. This class, Mrs. Laven was discussing the myth about Persephone. She was supposed to have been a beautiful girl kidnaped by the lord of the underworld and sent beneath the earth, only allowed to return in spring. The reason I was so fascinated by Persephone was that I felt my life was similar to hers. I felt that somewhere inside of me, the me I was supposed to be had been banished, was hiding inside of myself. But there was hope I'd find that self someday. The thought of my mother surfaced and I remembered what had happened the night before. I hoped she really had gone to the dentist as she had said she would, and that she wasn't in any more pain. The mother of Persephone was Demeter, the Earth Mother of the myth, and I wished I could bring Persephone's gift of rejuvenation to my own mother, to stop her from getting older.

Mrs. Laven let us out of mythology a few moments before the bell rang, so I waited for Nancy outside her geometry class. I could hear her teacher braying inside. Nancy's teacher was Mrs. Nerhew, and she had the loudest voice in the school. At the moment she was saying, "My head is on my shoulder, my shoulder isn't on my head." I didn't know what that meant, but it certainly sounded convincing to me.

Finally, the bell rang and Nancy came out the door.

"You got quite a workout," I said.

"She must have had a fight with her husband last night," Nancy said.

"We studied about a girl named Persephone today," I mentioned.

"Whoever she is," Nancy said, "I bet she has a lot more on the ball than *that* one"—she indicated Mrs. Nerhew sailing by.

"My dance class is at two-thirty today. When's yours?" I asked Nancy.

"Three-thirty at the Ballet Arts," she said. Nancy took lots of dance classes so she could perform ballet on ice.

"Let's have a soda after school at Rudley's," I said.

"Great."

We got into one of the school elevators that was so crowded we got out again and went up to biology class via the stairs. Biology was the most academic credit left in my program and the only class Nancy and I shared. A rock singer who had one of the top ten songs on the charts was gyrating to an inner tune as he went by us on the stairs. Nancy and I looked at him and smiled to each other.

The biology classroom smelled of formaldehyde

and I hated the smell. You never knew what was going to go on each day. Sometimes there would be a dissection of a cat or a demonstration of a fetal pig in a huge pickle jar. There was always a collection of tweezers and prodders lying around. Today we sat down and there was a chart of a human cell hanging in front of the blackboard. Nancy and I took our seats, which were right next to each other in the third row. Mrs. Phalan, the biology teacher, was busy preparing her notes for class. She had just had a baby during the summer, and during our unit on reproduction she actually brought the baby in. I had never held a baby so it had been a unique experience, although for the experienced baby-sitters in the crowd, I suppose, it was ordinary. I could feel the baby's little heart beating, and when I stroked the baby's head, I loved the warmth of his head and the softness of his hair. It gave me a lovely feeling.

"Okay, class," Mrs. Phalan said at the bell, "can we come to attention?" She coughed as though that would really help get the class's attention. Actually, Mrs. Phalan was very shy, and unfortunately some of the boys in the class took advantage of her and threw things at her. One kid once yelled out, "Hey, Mrs. Phalan, what species are you from?"

"Class," she said, coughing again, "yesterday we talked about the circulation of blood in the human being and today I wanted to get more specific and examine some of the components of blood, some of the specific cells which enable us to breathe and carry out our normal daily functions."

I hardly heard her because in addition to the fact that this class was one Nancy and I shared together, Brandon had a seat right behind me. The very first week he put a rubber frog down my back, and the next day he tied Nancy's hair into a mooring knot. He was always doing something crazy, but not mean, just silly to make us laugh. I turned my head. He was nibbling on a pencil. Linda, the daughter of a famous director, sat on my right, twisting her hair to get a frizzed effect. She was probably thinking about her next permanent. Scotty, who played Jungle Jim's son on a TV series that was getting a big run, was the only one I could see who looked attentive. Then there came a loud tapping sound. Mrs. Phalan was banging a stick against a chart on the blackboard. "This is the nucleus of a healthy cell," she was saying. "There are fifty trillion cells in the human body. More than all the people who are alive today. Most cells are so small that it would take ten thousand of them to cover the head of a pin," Mrs. Phalan added, as though she herself was responsible for the fact. "Our bodies are made of all different kinds of cells, but all cells live, grow and finally die."

Mrs. Phalan paused and then continued with excitement in her voice. It was cracking as though she was doing a dramatic performance. "The most exciting thing of all is that in the course of eight days there are all new cells in your body. So, in a manner of speaking, you are a totally new person every eight days."

Suddenly I was alert, intrigued by what Mrs. Phalan was saying. But a part of me was apprehensive about this discussion of nuclei and cells and blood. I was still thinking about my mother and all those "routine" tests. Something gnawed at me. Just something about vitamins, my father had said.

Mrs. Phalan hit the rubber tip of her pointer against the chart. I heard her saying, "When a cell divides, it is called mytosis." She continued, "And we're all the result of many healthy cells which are divided and specialized to form the various parts and organs of our bodies." I found myself hearing one particular word of her speech—"healthy"; *healthy* cells. Almost instinctively my hand shot up and I spoke before she even called on me.

"What's an *un*healthy cell?" I blurted.

"Why do you ask?"

"Because I'm interested," I said. "I was watching television last night and there was a story about a woman who was sick and got a pain in her mouth that made her cry and they were taking blood samples. The nurse in the program was talking about unhealthy cells."

Mrs. Phalan smiled with satisfaction as though Socratically she was leading me forth exactly as her lesson plan was designed. She pulled down a second chart and began waving her pointer almost joyfully.

"You're way ahead of us, Brooke," she said. "This chart shows unhealthy cells in the blood system. Notice the deterioration starts working its way into the center of the nucleus. Who can tell what makes that happen?" she asked the class.

"Some sort of bug," a kid yelled out from the back. But Mrs. Phalan was not amused.

"A disease," I said, seriously.

I could tell by the look on Mrs. Phalan's face she was annoyed because we weren't following parliamentary procedure. She could feel that the class was getting ready to go a little out of control, which happened at least a few times each period.

"That's right, Brooke," Mrs. Phalan said and looked toward some other kids, as though she wanted someone else besides me to contribute. *"But we must raise our hands before speaking,"* she said.

I raised my hand wildly, and since no one else seemed to be particularly awake, she had to call on me again.

"What is it, Brooke?"

"Is there any way you can make cells healthy again?" I asked. "I mean, someone who has *unhealthy* cells?" Mrs. Phalan looked at me. I was behaving out of character. She saw I was inordinately interested in the subject matter. To my surprise, she answered patiently.

"Well, sometimes you can take medication and sometimes doctors prescribe surgery," Mrs. Phalan answered.

By now I knew that Mrs. Phalan didn't want to hear my voice anymore, so I leaned over to Nancy and asked her to ask just one more question for me. Nancy looked at me, puzzled, but raised her hand.

"What is it, Nancy?" Mrs. Phalan inquired.

"Is there any time," Nancy started, faltering, and I had to whisper again the rest of the question: "when cells *stay* sick?" she completed, not even knowing why she was asking the question.

"There are," Mrs. Phalan answered, delighted that at last there was some other kid contributing to the discussion. "This is particularly true," she added, "in the case of cancerous cells."

The word "cancerous" riveted me. I felt as though my chest was collapsing. The next second I was crying. I lowered my head. I didn't want Nancy to see me. I didn't want anyone to see me. I raised my right hand to cover my face, and then my left, and I lowered myself down into my seat. I had both hands up to my forehead as though shielding my eyes from the light, pretending to be absorbed. Then I began to shake and the book fell from my hands to the floor. I picked it up but Nancy saw something was wrong. I turned my face to the right. I could think of nothing now but Mom and the sudden pain which had made her cry at the dinner table. I felt someone tapping me on the shoulder. My body was shaking and I turned my head just slightly to see Brandon reaching out to me.

"What's the matter?" he asked in a gentle voice.

I couldn't talk, I didn't want to talk because talking about it would make it realer and there'd be no turning back.

"My mother has cancer," I said, flatly, trying to turn into a stone in my seat, a stone that wouldn't feel or be hurt or break in front of the class.

"How do you know?" Brandon asked.

He handed me a tissue to wipe my face. Then Nancy leaned over. "What's the matter, Brooke?" Mrs. Phalan was so intent she didn't notice us. She'd returned to the topic of nuclei and mytosis and white blood corpuscles and little fragments that float about the circulatory system waiting to wedge and weave a clot to heal all wounds.

"Maybe you're wrong," Brandon whispered in my ear. He kept his hand touching my shoulder, and his touch comforted me.

The boy who played Jungle Jim's son kept staring, but he didn't say anything. Nancy opened her large loose-leaf book and moved as though she was sharing it with me, hoping to protect me from the stares of others. But I didn't care. I knew my mother was going to die.

3

I caught the 4:09 train home from Pennsylvania Station. I felt an inner exhaustion that was different from any I had ever had from dance class. I walked the six blocks home. I turned the corner to my street and went up the pink pavement path which led to our back door. My mother's face was still in my mind. I didn't want her to see that I was frightened.

I slowed, then went up the three steps to the side door, which was nestled behind a large peach tree my brother had planted from a pit years before when he was too lazy to throw it in the garbage can. Its orange-colored leaves had already turned a muted yellow. I opened the back door and walked in. The smell of roast lamb filled the kitchen.

"Just in time for supper," my mother said. She came to me giving me a gentle kiss and a big hug which was softened from the thickness of my green blazer. "The lamb chops are still pink," she added, turning back to melting butter on the stove. "Did you have a hard class?" she asked, all a little too quickly, as if she was as nervous as I was. When my mother got nervous her eyes blinked an extra few times.

"How's your tooth?" I asked.

"Fine," Mom said. "It hurts a little, but it's on the mend. I've made myself some mashed potatoes, but don't worry—I've got French fries and Brussels sprouts for you kids."

My father arrived home a few minutes later and we all sat down at the table. Dinnertime was an important event at our house. My mother made a geat effort to make it fun. My father took the seat of honor at the Formica table, the chair from which he had a good view out the window. He was the one who always seemed to have the energy. He'd jump up if you needed a spoon or a fork or help my mother with anything she needed, no matter how hard he had worked all day. Anytime I ever asked him if he was tired, he'd always say, "What? *Me, tired?* I'm ready to hit Coney Island." And then he'd laugh. Sometimes when company was over he'd tell us again the story about when he and Mom got on the parachute ride in a rainstorm.

During dinner that night, I tried to avoid looking at my mother. Pete took a big bowl of French fries and passed it along family style. No one said very much. Then my father took the platter of lamb chops.

"Does anyone else want meat?" he asked. He loved to see us eat. This was probably a throwback to when he had just come with his parents and seven brothers and sisters from Europe and there wasn't enough food for them. However, our refrigerator on Long Island was overflowing.

"Brooke, you're awfully quiet," my mother said softly.

"I'm all right, Mom," I said.

"How was school?" she probed.

"Great," I said. "We talked about Persephone, the goddess of spring."

"No kidding," Pete said. "I just met her last week down at the pizza parlor. She ordered a large to go with everything on it."

We all laughed, and then I reminded everyone about last year's spring when we woke up one day and just decided to ride out to Montauk Point and pick wild flowers. "Let's do it again next spring, okay, Mom?"

My mother looked at me, and her face seemed to lose a shade of color. She took a sip of water and smiled at me.

"We'll see," she said. "That would be nice." She got up from the table and started getting a pile of laundry together. She opened my schoolbag and threw my leotards and tights into the heap. "I'm really not very hungry," she said, grabbing a box of Tide from under the kitchen sink.

I looked at my father and I could see he was unsure what to do. He turned to my brother.

"Pete," he said, "Mom told me your application for admission came from Farmingdale Agricultural College. What do you say we fill it out tonight?"

"Thanks, Dad," Pete said, "but I don't know if that's the right place for me."

"Of course it's right for you," Dad insisted.

"But I don't want to be a farmer," Pete said. "At least, I don't *think* I want to be."

He got up from the table. "Well, if you'll excuse me, folks, I've got a date with the boob tube." He marched out into the living room.

By the time I finished eating, my mother had gone down to the basement to load up the washing machine and do some ironing. I helped my father clear the dishes off the table—that was my responsibility. My other job was setting the table whenever I got home early enough. Pete was assigned to garbage, a detail that needed attending to later on in the evening and that he usually did on his way out to a bar. My father rolled up his sleeves and started washing the dishes. He always did them.

I was wiping off the table with a sponge, automatically, like a robot. There was only one thing on my mind and I decided that I would find that out from my father. "Dad," I finally said, "can I ask you something?"

"Shoot," he said, rinsing the suds out of the blender. "What is it?"

"Well, Dad," I started, "Mom hasn't been looking too well lately." I didn't know how the words managed to get past the lump in my throat.

Dad put some scouring powder in the big old frying pan and was scrubbing it hard. The scratching, which used to send chills up my spine, didn't seem grating at this moment.

"Mom went to the doctor today and he said she might need some treatments, but there was nothing to worry about."

My father had never lied to me, but this time I didn't believe him.

"But Dad," I pursued, "Mom always seems a little sick. A little tired. And what about her tooth last night at dinner? Why was there so much pain?"

He slowed down the scrubbing.

"Your mother's been feeling a little sick lately, Brooke, that's true," he said sadly. "But the doctors say they're very optimistic about her future and she's going to be fine." His voice cracked a little.

"Dad, please, if there's anything I should know, I think you should tell me. She seems *different*," I said, pleading. "Please don't treat me like a child. Mom is in pain, Daddy, I know that. Maybe I can help. She's always been there for me. Maybe I can be there for her now."

My father listened and I couldn't tell if he was going to tell me anything. This is one of the awful things about being a kid. They deny your right to know what is happening. They try to protect you when they can't.

"I want to know!" I said more forcefully. "I have a right to know. Don't close me out."

My father kept rinsing the dishes and placing them in the dishwasher, forming a rhythmic beat as one dish hit against the rest.

"Look, Brooke, your mom's not young anymore. She's forty-five years old and you can't expect her to have the same kind of energy as when she was forty."

Oh, Dad, I said to myself, *if only I could believe you.* I wanted desperately to believe him, but I couldn't.

Then a silence filled the kitchen. All I could hear was the water running out of the spout at full force, and I knew that for once my father's mind was not on water conservation and that only made me more afraid. Finally, he turned and looked at me.

"You know, Brooke, you never cease to surprise me," he said. He put his arm around me.

I relished the safety of his touch. It reminded me that I loved my father very much.

"In biology class today," I told him, "Mrs. Phalan talked about cancerous cells. I'm scared. Is that what's wrong with Mom?"

My father loosened his embrace, walked to the sink and dried his hands on the towel. He needed to turn his face away from me.

"Now, now, sweetheart," he said, starting to dry the pots, "nothing is going to happen to Mom, do you hear that? She's got a lot of fight in her." And then he came back to me and kissed me on the top of my head.

This time I hugged him as hard as I could.

"Thanks, Dad," I finally said. I started out of the kitchen and I could see my father was very upset.

In the living room I rummaged through some rows of books until I found our medical dictionary, which was pretty well worn. My parents used it for everything from diagnosing colds to typhoid fever.

Many times when no one was home, I would take it to my room and look up scientific definitions, things like menstruation, sexual intercourse, ovulation, sperm count. This time, I was carrying the book upstairs for a different quest. Closing the door of my room behind me, I lay down on my bed and quickly turned to the subject of *cancer*. There was a lot of information, almost eight pages on that topic alone, and after reading it I found it really wasn't specific enough for me to know anything more than I had suspected. Then I went to the bathroom medicine cabinet and read the labels on all of my mother's medicine bottles. There were a few new ones and the names were very complicated. One said something like "corteoplastic." . . . I ran quickly back to the dictionary before forgetting the name and turned, flying, through the pages looking to see what it was. I saw the words "cobalt treatment" and I remembered my mother's sister, who had died of cancer several years ago. Just then the phone rang in my room. The phone had been my birthday gift the year before with my own private number, the best birthday present I'd ever gotten. I picked up the yellow receiver.

"Hello, Brooke?" I heard at the other end. My heart almost stopped when I realized it was Brandon's voice.

"Did you speak to your mom?" he asked.

"No," I told him. "I asked my father."

"What'd he say?" Brandon pursued anxiously. His voice seemed filled with concern for me.

"He said not to worry."

"See? I told you so."

"Maybe," I added.

"Say"—he changed his tone—"say, I was thinking, we're putting our boat in retirement for the winter, but my mother said I could have a last boat ride. Do you want to go out Saturday afternoon?"

I was so surprised I didn't know what to say. A boat ride seemed incongruous considering the medical dictionary I was still holding.

My heart began to beat very fast. I couldn't tell whether this was a date out of pity or whether he had meant to call me and see me and that it took an event like this for us to talk. Maybe my father *had* been telling me the truth, maybe my mom was okay! Maybe there was no reason to worry about anything. It was wonderful hearing Brandon's voice! If I was blindfolded in a room of a hundred people, I could find my way to him just by the fullness of his voice.

"I'd love to," I said. "I haven't been on an Indian summer boat ride for quite a while." I didn't want him to know that I had never in my life been on any kind of a boat ride with a boy, except when I took a canoe test at camp when I was twelve. Life is really funny. When everything seems to be falling apart, something good happens.

"By the way," he added, "I auditioned for a movie."

"Nancy told me about it," I let him know.

"Well, I *got* it," he said, joyously. *"I got the part."*

"That's great!" I said. "What's it about?"

"It's about two brothers going West. I play the younger one. The sensitive one."

"Typecasting," I retorted, and we laughed together.

"They don't start shooting for another month, so I won't have to go to Hollywood for a while," he added, as if a month was a long time.

And then I felt a familiar flash of inadequacy, a need to exaggerate about my own life.

"My mother and I will be going out to California right after graduation. She thinks I have a good chance out there." Actually, that wasn't a total lie, I told myself, waiting for his response. My mother did think I stood a good chance in Hollywood, but who knew if we would really go?

"Great," Brandon said.

"Wouldn't that be something if we all wound up in Hollywood!" I said.

"You'll be there," Brandon insisted, filling me with encouragement. "Are you going to the audition for the new *Lassie* TV special?"

"What *Lassie* TV special?" I asked.

"It's on the bulletin board at school," Brandon said, surprised I hadn't noticed. "It went up this afternoon. They want a girl who can dance."

"Oh, thanks. I'll look at it tomorrow," I said. "Maybe I will if I can get my act together."

"I think they want to audition in November. That gives you long enough."

"Yes, it does."

"Good. See you at school tomorrow, and then on

Saturday my mother will drive me over to pick you up for the boat ride." Suddenly, having Brandon come over to pick me up frightened me. The hours spent daydreaming about the special boy coming around for me were actually happening now, but Brandon wasn't just the boy next door.

"Oh, *no*," I stopped him. The thought that he had more money than my family, that he lived in a big apartment in New York and had a country home on Long Island Sound, made me afraid he'd think my home was too simple. I hated myself for feeling ashamed of where I came from but the words had shot out. "My mother can drive me."

"You sure?"

"Sure, I'm sure," I said.

"Great." And then he added, "In fact, maybe your mom could have lunch with mine at the Yacht Club while we're out in the boat."

"That sounds terrific. I'll ask her," I said gratefully.

"Good night," he said.

"Good night, Brandon." I waited to hear him hang up the phone first, just in case he had any last message. I hated saying good-bye. I became aware of the weight of the dictionary crushing my ribs. I took it off my chest and just stared at the dark cover. Then I heard my mother and father whispering in their bedroom across the hall. They had closed their door, which was unusual for this time of the evening. Anything private they had to say they usually saved until my brother and I had gone to bed, but sometimes when I couldn't fall asleep I'd hear whispers coming from their bedroom. I always wondered what married people talked about in the dark. Sometimes it seemed that they talked more before going to sleep than they did for the entire day. Maybe there's something about the dark that makes it easier to talk. It seems like a really nice thing to do and maybe someday I'll be able to be in the dark with someone, too, lying side by side, listening, caring about feelings, someone to touch in every way.

Then I heard Pete yelling to my parents' room.

"See you later," Pete said.

"Where you going?" my father asked.

"Scotty's," Pete said, going down the steps.

"The gin mill again?"

"They sell *pizza*, too. I'm going for *pizza*," he said.

"You're not driving," my father bellowed.

"Don't sweat it," Pete yelled up, "my friends are picking me up."

"Okay," my father acquiesced. "Just make sure you don't ram your fist through a glass door again."

I heard Pete slam the downstairs door. My father went back to the bedroom and I heard him whisper a minute longer with my mother. Then he went downstairs. After a moment, I heard my mother's voice calling me from her room. She had a soft voice.

"Brooke, could you come in here for a moment?" she called.

I heard her but I didn't move.

"Brooke," she called a little louder, "would you come in for a minute—I want to talk to you."

Slowly, I got up off my bed and moved to open the door of my room. I went forward. I stood at the entrance of her room, unable to walk farther. I stared at the rose-colored patterns on the wallpaper. My mother was lying in bed, her head resting on several pillows. The lamp on her bedstand made a soft glow around her face. She looked very pretty. Even without makeup, her light skin and her dark hair complemented her blue eyes. Her eyes looked very blue and very strong, and I turned away because her glance was too knowing, too understanding.

"What is it, Mom?" I asked slowly.

"Here," she said, patting the bed. "Sit down here. I want to talk to you."

Moments ago I had been begging my father for the truth, but now I felt afraid. I broke out in a cold sweat. I was sure she heard the pounding in my chest, because that's all I could hear. She looked right at me and I looked straight back at her. *Mom, what is happening?* I wanted to cry out. *Please give me* strength *to be able to sit next to you and listen.*

"Brooke, what I've got to tell you is one of the hardest things I've ever had to do," she said.

I felt myself cutting off, freezing. The pounding stopped. "What is it, Mom?" I said.

My mother paused a moment and looked down. Slowly, her eyes met mine and neither of us turned away.

"Brooke, what I have, you don't get better from," she said. "Do you understand what I'm trying to tell you?" she said, urging me to understand.

All I could do was shake my head no. I said, "No."

"Brooke, please, you're making it harder for me than it already is."

I kept shaking my head. "No, I don't understand." But the problem was I understood too well and couldn't accept it.

"Brooke, I'm very sick. I have cancer. I'm going to die."

"No," I cried, and fell into her arms. She held me tightly and I clung to her and we cried together.

"It's good to cry sometimes," she said finally.

"Mom, I don't want you to die. I don't want you to leave us. We need you. I need you. I love you so!"

"I know," my mother said as she stroked my hair. "I know. And I love you more than you could know," she said as she reached over and pulled out some tissues and we both tried drying our tears. I could sense what a great relief it was for my mother to be rid of the burden she had been carrying around, wondering when and how she should tell me.

The blinds were shut, and only the light coming in between the slats from the street made me aware of the outside world. How many times that streetlight had guided me in the middle of the night as I found my way to my mother's bed and reached out for my mother's warmth. She would pull me up, tucking the comforter around me, and she'd hold me close to her till morning. Tonight the light didn't help me find my way at all.

"You know, Brooke, I can't accept the fact that at some point I will never see you again. Or Pete or Dad.

I still can't comprehend that," my mother confessed. She put her hands over her eyes. "But I had to know the truth. I told the doctor to tell me and he did. If I was dying, I had to know. There were plans to be made and time would become different for me."

"What did he tell you?" I asked.

"He said I had bone cancer and that it had already started spreading. He said it was inoperable. That means it's only a matter of time."

"How could that be?" I said incredulously. "Last year you had a checkup and you were fine."

"This time I wasn't so lucky," she said. "After he told me, I wandered aimlessly around the streets letting the fact sink in. Some man stopped me and asked if I was all right. Then I came home. No one was here, and I felt terribly alone. I really wanted one of you to be here. Then I came up to my room and started going through old papers, letters you and Pete had sent from camp, even the first Mother's Day card you made for me from school. I'm not ready to say good-bye, Brooke." Mom started to cry again.

"How can you ever get ready to say good-bye?" I said, taking her hand in mine. "I'll never be ready to say good-bye to you." Tears rolled down my face.

"Then we both must prepare for it," she said with determination, as if she had rehearsed it all in her mind all those sleepless nights.

"How do you do that?" I desperately asked her, the person who always knew the answers.

"The first step is knowing the truth, then we go on from there," she said.

"Go on? On to where?" I said, searching her eyes for some hidden meaning.

"I'm trying to accept it, Brooke, and so must you. We are born and we die, and what we do in between is called living, and that is what counts. Brooke, I'm going to do it while I'm still here. But I need your help. Will you help me, Brooke?"

"Of course I'll help you. I'll do anything," I said as I sat there in shock and awe. In spite of what my mother knew, she was imbued with an energy I had never quite seen in her before. I remembered how dynamic she was as the first woman president of the local Democratic club and as president of the P.T.A. Now I realized she had taken over the helm of a new group called "Live Today Now." Through her tears shone a strength that would become her lifeline.

"How can I help, tell me?!" I asked her.

She wiped some tears and looked into my eyes. Then a smile started forming at the end of her lips, a tender smile that she got when she was sure she knew the answer and wanted to share it with you.

"Don't mourn for me now, honey, I'm still here. We have to work very hard and fast, make every minute count."

What did she mean? I wondered as she read the expression on my face.

"You're a very special girl, and you were meant for great things. I'm proud of who you are," my mother said. "You've made me very happy. You've been the greatest joy in my life, Brooke—and I know you'll continue to make me very proud of you."

"Oh Mom," I said. "I'll try to be everything you want." But deep inside I wasn't sure I could be all that. Suddenly this great responsibility of making my mother happy consumed me and I thought of Pete. "Have you told Pete yet?" I asked, wondering if everyone in the house knew this secret except me.

"What happened was unfortunate." My mother winced with guilt. "A few weeks ago I sent Pete to the supermarket for some milk and he overheard Mrs. Samuels—you know, the one who yells when the kids run on her lawn. She said to the lady who checks us out, 'Isn't it a shame about Claire, she's so young. But she's got a lot of fight in her.' Mrs. Samuels does volunteer work at the hospital and is very nosy.

"Pete came home terribly upset, in shock. 'What's going on?' he asked me in tears. 'What do you mean?' I asked him. He told me what he overheard. It was then that I told him the truth, like I'm telling you now. And when I told him, he cried like a baby. It's the first time I've seen him cry since he was ten years old. Then he looked at me. 'Why didn't you tell me, Mom? Why did I have to find out from a stranger in the supermarket?'

"He was hurt and he had a right to be, but I just wasn't ready to talk about it yet. He found out too soon."

"I understand, Mom," I said, trying to ease her penitence. I thought how direct Pete was that he could speak out freely what was on his mind. I could never have confronted her as Pete had. I admired Pete for that. If my mother hadn't called me into her room this evening, I know I would not have had the courage to ask her what was going on. I had asked my father instead.

"Maybe in the time I have left, I'll get a chance to see some of your success," she said hopefully.

"You will, Mom, I promise you," I found myself saying, wanting to please her.

She smiled. "Perhaps you can be all that I couldn't be," she said vulnerably.

"Did *you* ever want to be a star?" I asked.

She thought a moment, then answered, "I suppose I wanted to accomplish great things, but my mother never made me feel like I was somebody. Maybe I never believed enough in myself. My mother never expected great things from me. Oh, Brooke." She sighed. "It's you I will miss most of all."

She took me in her arms and rocked me like a baby. And as she rocked me, the softness of her breasts brought back a rush of memories of all the times I had run into her arms when I was a little girl, and later when I was hurt or disappointed. I thought about my mother when she was a little girl and wondered if her mother had held her the same way she was holding me now. My eyes fell upon the pearl ring surrounded by diamonds Mother always wore. Her mother had given it to her on her eighteenth birthday. I wondered, as these feelings of comfort and stroking from my mother poured into me, if this unspoken dialogue was passed on from generation to generation. Would I someday hold my daughter as my mother was holding me right now? And as she gently rocked me in her arms, I felt my mind drift off to yet another place. A little voice in me wanted to say, *Mom. Forgive me! I'm not special in the way you want me to be. I don't want to feel guilty going out with Brandon and wanting something real, something more exciting than the audition for* Lassie *that's coming up.* I didn't want want to feel guilty that I wasn't special in the way my mother wanted me to be.

And as she stroked the back of my hair, I wanted to ask her what good having great success was if I came home to an empty house with no one to share my joy and excitement, no one to hold me like she was holding me right this moment? I think that if I was successful, I'd feel the loneliness that much more if I didn't have anyone to share it with. Many of the people who want to be stars, what they really want to feel is love. I've read about famous people who finally achieved their greatest life's ambition, then came home and killed themselves because they were alone, devastatingly alone. Maybe if they had had someone to share their victories with, someone who could hold them tenderly like my mother was holding me now, their lives might have had different endings. I wanted to whisper, safely there in my mother's wings, *I don't want to be like them, feeling an emptiness in my stomach, never peaceful, always searching, hoping that tomorrow on the bus, or walking down the block, I will meet the right one who will fill me with a sense of completion. I know I can have a career and perhaps be a success which will fulfill a part of me, but I want something real and lasting, and that means someone's love. And Mom, I know I must be right because why does it feel so good to be right here in your arms? I don't want to settle for anything less. It isn't that I just want to be someone's wife, or just be a success. I want to be myself and that is the hardest job of all.*

Unlike Pete, I couldn't speak my mind, and if ever I wanted to please my mother, it was now. So I finally spoke out. "We'll make every day count, I promise, Mom. You will be proud of me," I said softly.

4

"Up and at it! Up and at it!" My mother's voice came floating up the stairs. It was a voice determined to make every day count.

The sun was filtering through my white shutters when I heard Mom's call. This morning I was glad to hear it. It was seven-fifteen. Somehow I had managed to sleep through lots of nightmares. I didn't want to remember any of them, but one in particular continued to haunt me. The feeling from the dream made my body shake. In the dream I was wearing the pearl ring my mother always wore. The one given to her by my grandmother. I was walking home from school and looked down at the ring, which was now on my finger, and the pearl in the center was missing. I had *lost* the pearl. Frantically, I started running back toward the train, following my footsteps, searching everywhere for the lost stone, but I couldn't find it anywhere. My search became more frantic; I searched every corner, every niche. Everywhere I looked, I couldn't find the white pearl. I knew I had lost it forever. I fell down onto the ground, unable to move or speak. At that moment I woke up and felt tears falling down my cheek. As I wiped the tears away with the back of my hand, I was astonished that the tears had broken through the barriers of my dreams and become real. Before, when I had cried in a dream it had stayed in the dream. This was the first time a nightmare had pervaded my waking life. I blinked a few times to see if even now I was still dreaming, but then I heard my brother open the side door downstairs and I knew I was in my bedroom. Quickly I pulled my hand out from under the blanket and there really was no ring. I hadn't lost any pearl. I was relieved. I don't know which nightmare was greater, staying awake or sleeping, so when my mother's voice called up, I was grateful we'd both made it through another night.

I opened my closet to find something to wear. I had a great walk-in closet filled with clothes and junk for any mood. I remembered the hours when I was a little kid and kept my dolls in there. My friends would come over and we'd get dressed up in all sorts of outfits and pretend we were everyone from Marie Antoinette to Diana Ross. When I got older, sometimes we'd play post office in the closet with boys. Many times, through the years, I had just gone into the closet, closed the door and cried when I hadn't wanted anyone to find me. I had done a lot of laughing and crying in that closet and, in a funny way, my closet had shared my life with me more than any of my friends.

This morning I had to share another secret with it as I looked for something to wear.

And as I searched the rainbow of blouses, it dawned on me that in the dream the center of the ring was my mother, and it was her that I was desperately searching for through the streets. I stood in the closet filled with clothes and shoes, and junk, and old toys, necklaces hanging on a rack and hats scattered haphazardly, and I screamed out, "I am being deserted! Do you hear me, somebody, I am being deserted!" Quickly I covered my mouth with my hand, almost shocked that the words had come out in the first place. I put on an old green bulky sweater, one that wasn't particularly flattering but very comfortable. I didn't care how I looked today. I zippered up a plaid skirt my mother had bought me at Bloomingdale's and went downstairs.

During breakfast, my mother and I didn't mention the night before. I did tell her about the *Lassie* auditions—and I asked if I could go out on Brandon's boat on Saturday and she said it would be fine. She said she *would* drive me, and if Brandon's mother wanted to invite her to lunch at the Yacht Club that would be just fine, too.

I grabbed my tote bag and Mom slipped a chocolate bar in.

"Quick energy for your dance class," she said. "It'll help you fly during your round-off flip-flops." We both laughed as I opened the back door and started down the steps.

"You know, Brooke"—my mother's voice stopped me—"I think you're going to have to start taking an extra speech class every week. Yesterday I read in the paper that they're doing a version of *Carousel* down at the Civic Theater, and I think it wouldn't hurt if you tried out for it. You could audition with your number from *Slaughter on Tenth Avenue.*"

"That's a good idea," I said, remembering the promise I'd made to her last night to fulfill her wish in the time we had left.

Then without even pausing to breathe, she said, "Do you know what kind of girl they want for the *Lassie* TV special?"

"Nope. But I'll find out," I said assuringly.

"If it's a country girl, I want you to look the part. Maybe we could pigtail your hair. I'll look through your closet and see if there's anything that will look right. Maybe that green straw hat. They always have that around Lassie, always the country image."

"Mom, I don't know what type they're looking for, but they're mainly going to want to see me dance at the audition."

"You're being very naive," Mom said. "Dancing is only a part of it. They have to like you before you even start dancing. The first impression is crucial."

"Okay, Mom, anything you say." Then I turned around the hedges and headed for school. A voice inside me seemed to say, *Remember, action now. Not tomorrow, not next year. Action* now.

I jogged to the train, thinking about my mother's last remarks. It was curious to me that she could be thinking of me at a time like this. How much she must want me to succeed for her. I fought to hold back fresh tears. I wondered whether, if I knew *I* was going to disappear, *I* was going to die, I could still care about being a star.

I got on the train and it snaked its way to Manhattan. Then I transferred to the noisy subway. But for some reason I got off at the stop before my regular one. I came up onto Fiftieth Street went across on the tiny block between Broadway and Seventh Avenue and walked up Seventh toward Carnegie Hall. There was a small movie house there and I noticed it was showing an old movie of Marilyn Monroe's. To me, Marilyn Monroe was the most beautiful actress who ever lived. And suddenly I wanted to see her. It was almost ten o'clock in the morning and the box office was open. I was surprised it was open that early. Then I saw a sign, "Special Senior Citizen Performance." I paid a little old lady in the booth and found myself inside the theater. It was then that I worried about Nancy waiting for me on the corner, but I knew she would figure out I wasn't coming to school this morning.

The movie began and there was Marilyn up there on the screen, bigger than life, and she was moving in that sensuously innocent way she had. She was beautiful as always. She had that face, those eyes, the adoration of so many men wanting her; and whenever I saw her I wished that someday I would be like her. Then I remembered she grew up in an orphanage because her mother hadn't wanted her. No matter how much money and success she had, Marilyn wasn't supposed to have been very happy. *A star needs someone who really believes in her,* I thought, and then wondered about the people around Marilyn who made her grow into what she became. A star and a suicide. I found my thoughts drifting to my mother, about evenings when I would go out on a date, how I would ask her, "Mom, do I look all right?"

"Of course you look all right, sweetheart. You're a beautiful girl," she'd say. But I never felt beautiful.

She'd be sitting in the living room reading or watching television in her special chair, or sewing or just talking with my father. And she would catch me looking at myself in the hallway mirror trying to analyze my profile and small chin. She'd always catch me.

"No," she'd say. "You can look from now till doomsday, but you have to feel pretty inside," she'd say, pointing toward her heart.

"I know that," I said defensively, many times. But I didn't know how to find that place she was pointing to.

A close shot of Marilyn came on the screen, and her look was gentle, like that of a young girl in a grown-up body. It was as though she was smiling right at me, and the shot of her face, although fleeting on the screen, seemed frozen in time. Marilyn was smiling and telling me a secret. I think there are a few times in your life when some sort of truth comes thundering down on you, and on this day, in that little theater, I thought that this was one of those times. Marilyn Monroe, behind the pounds of heavy masking powder and magical Hollywood lashes, was peering outside her image and looking right at me, Brooke Hillary, and telling me something so real that it was frightening. I could see that she had another life beneath that veneer. What she really had to say was more of a scream. Marilyn had had acting teachers tell her what to do, people who invited her to stay at their houses, men who married her, men and all of Hollywood to tell her who she was and what she had to be. But she was something else underneath, someone I saw for a second when she smiled.

Underneath this successful star was an unsuccessful woman who committed suicide. She must have been very lonely, no matter how much adoration she received. I have read that sometimes people attempt to take their own lives as a last desperate try to call out, "Somebody help me! I need help!" No one had heard her calling out. Maybe no one had been listening to her calls for a long time. Marilyn might not have met the end she did if people hadn't tried to make her into something she wasn't. According to an article I read about her, she was very shy and it took her three hours to get dressed and put on her makeup just so she would look like the person we knew as Marilyn Monroe. She must have been a very different person from the Hollywood image she portrayed. I couldn't help wondering what would I be like without my mother's voice charting my steps.

Brooke, we have an audition for you for The King and I *Tuesday.—Brooke, I think we should throw in an extra voice lesson, because the City Opera is doing a revival of* West Side

Story.—*Brooke, I hear there's an opening for the understudy part in the road company of* The Prime of Miss Jean Brodie.*—Brooke, I'll meet you in New York on Wednesday to get new toe shoes.—Brooke, you've got to lose five pounds.— Brooke, you're eating too much.—Brooke, your face looks too full.—Brooke, you can't go ice skating with the kids because you can't afford to break your ankle.*

If my mother was to die, that voice would disappear—and even though I hated to think of the pain my mother might have to go through, her anguish and torment to come, there was a part of me that was terrified for myself. I could hear this frightened voice of my own saying, *I don't want to take another dance class. I don't want any more auditions. I don't want any more rejections. I don't think I can do any of this on my own.* Then I paused a moment and thought, *What would be so terrible if I wasn't a star? Could someone love me as I am? Unadorned, untinseled? Could someone love plain Brooke, Claire's daughter, the one who is sort of pretty who lives in the corner house on Norma Street? Could someone love that girl?* What if I shouldn't become a star while my mother was here to enjoy it? Would I really want it for *ME?* Thump. A divider came down, closing me off from any feeling, and all I could see was the trivia: Did I give the record I borrowed back to Nancy? Which night did I wash my hair? But then, like a major theme returning in a symphony, my mother's voice came into my consciousness again.

You want me to be proud of you, Brooke, don't you? You're going to be a star, Brooke. You're going to be the first star that ever came out of the Hillary family. You're going to be the first one to finish what you started. You're not going to drop out like your father. You're not going to drop out like Pete. You're going to climb on all our shoulders. You're going to use all our energy.

I found myself leaping up out of the theater seat, running out onto the street and hurrying to school.

5

"Brandon. Brandon," I called out as I ran up the five flights of stairs. The bell had just rung and Brandon was coming out of history class.

"Brandon, I've got to talk to you," I said, pulling him off to a corner of the hall, out of the line of traffic.

"What is it?" he said with some alarm.

"My mother. She *is* dying. I knew it. I just knew it," I said, my voice cracking. I needed someone out there who cared enough to listen.

He took my hand and looked down. "I'm sorry, Brooke." His touch made me able to talk.

"Nothing makes any sense to me anymore," I said. "My world is caving in."

He put his hand on my shoulder. "I'm here," he said. His hand felt strong and I closed my eyes. His reaching out for me at that moment seemed an unbreakable bond, as if his words were a promise signed in blood.

The kids were all running into the next class.

"I was worried about you all last night," he said in a soft voice. Now the entire hall was clear except for us standing there in the empty green hallway.

Then the bell rang.

How I hated the shrill bell that interrupts our normal beats in life as it breaks up time each day, Monday to Friday, terminating one class, beginning another. Measuring minutes for biology, history, French, but not measuring important moments in people's lives.

I hated to leave Brandon.

"See you later," he said, as we both headed toward different classrooms.

Thursday afternoon in the school lunchroom, Nancy was trying to bring me up to date for a biology test.

I had told her about my mother the day before.

"Hey, Brooke, you're not listening to a word I'm saying."

"I'm sorry, Nancy. I was just thinking about an audition. About *Slaughter.*"

"You're a smash with that number. You've done *Slaughter on Tenth Avenue* so many times," she said encouragingly.

"But it's more important this time," I explained.

"I know," she said. "Brooke, when you told me about your mother, I didn't say much. I didn't know what to say. I can't believe your mother is dying. If it was my mother, I think I would go crazy."

"Nancy, I don't know what to do. I can't seem to

hold it all together. I'm not that strong," I said.

"Yes you are," Nancy said. "Isn't it incredible, Brooke, in biology class you just *knew* the truth?"

"I suppose I knew at some level," I agreed. "But to really know is different. What do I do, Nancy? What do I do?"

"Brooke," Nancy said sympathetically, "I think when something like this comes up you've got to pray for a miracle."

"You know something, Nancy," I said, "my mother has more energy than ever. She's determined to make the most out of each day for both of us. She's even arranging voice classes for me. I'm the one who's depressed. She's fighting on."

"Then she hasn't given up?" Nancy asked.

"She's more determined than ever to live," I answered.

"Boy, she's got guts," Nancy said.

"And she's feeling well enough to drive me to Brandon's house on Saturday, and you know what else? She's going to have lunch with Brandon's mother at the club, and she's looking forward to it."

"I told you he liked you," Nancy said.

"Oh Nancy," I answered, with part embarrassment and part delight. But then I felt a tinge of self-doubt. "Maybe he invited me out of pity because he feels sorry for me."

"Maybe he likes you," Nancy corrected.

I waited to the end of the week for Brandon to confirm our date for Saturday. Each time we passed each other in the hall, we would just smile quickly, and when there was a free moment, there were always other kids around. I wanted to say, "Hey, everybody, just leave us alone for a minute. We have something to talk about." I was beginning to get nervous about the audition for the *Lassie* special even though it was months away. Once my mother and I had gotten the actual date, we started rehearsing *Slaughter on Tenth Avenue*. I suppose concentrating on me helped her forget.

Friday Nancy and I were having lunch together.

"Brooke, look who just came into the cafeteria," Nancy whispered animatedly. "No, don't turn around now," she added.

"Who is it?" I begged. "Who is it? Is it who I think it is?"

"Yes," she said. "You can look now."

I turned and saw Brandon looking around the room until his eyes seemed to focus on a table. He went to sit with a dark-haired boy, the son of the stripper, who was wolfing down a sandwich.

"Talk to me," Nancy said. "We'll pretend we don't even know he's there. That should get his attention."

"He's eating his hamburger."

"Maybe he was waiting for you to look back," Nancy suggested. "Maybe he's looking for some sign of encouragement to come over. Why don't you start eating your hamburger, that will look casual."

"Shh," I said, "do you think he heard us?"

Nancy said, "I don't think he heard anything."

"He looks very intense."

"Yes," I said, actually thinking how virile he was.

Suddenly, before I could stop Nancy, she was waving and I froze in horror as I realized she was waving at Brandon to come over. I couldn't even speak. Nancy had a wicked smile on her face, and then Brandon was right there at our table. I could have killed her and kissed her at the same time.

"Mind if I sit down?" Brandon asked.

"No," Nancy said quickly. "We were hoping you would."

I was so embarrassed I couldn't even look at either of them as they exchanged a few jokes. After what seemed like a second Nancy had gobbled down the rest of her lunch and was standing up. "Well, if you'll excuse me," Nancy said, "I've got to make a phone call before French class." She swooped her tray off the table and headed out the door.

Brandon and I both sat there eating our lunch without saying a word, and I felt as though we had been married for years and didn't have to talk to feel a sense of togetherness, like my parents, after the nighttime chores were completed and the dishwasher turned on, signaling the end of a day's work. They felt secure enough with each other just to sit in the same room and not say a word. Each other's presence was enough to make them feel content.

After what seemed like four hours had passed, I said, "How do you feel about silence?"

"Silence never bothered me," he said. "Sometimes I like it. I mean, I never felt I had to talk just to break a silence, did you?"

"No," I said, "there's something nice about being with someone and not having to talk. Married people do that for years."

We both burst into laughter.

"Sometimes silences are very full," I added.

"That's right, like a pregnant pause," he said, smiling. "How's everything at home?" he said, changing his tone.

"My mother seems to be doing remarkably well. It amazes me the fight she has in her."

"You've inherited her spunkiness," he said with a smile.

"I have?" I said, enjoying the compliment.

"Are we still going out tomorrow?" he asked.

Could he imagine that I might have changed my mind?

"Of course," I said.

"Let's get an early start," he said. "I spoke to my mother and she'd really like it if your mother would spend the day with her. She's going to call her tonight and make it official."

Brandon's mother and my mother *did* know each other superficially from P.T.A. meetings, but that was all.

"Does your mother know about my mother?" I asked.

"Yes," he said. "Is that all right?"

"Yes," I told him. "It's not a secret anymore."

On Saturday morning I opened my eyes and ran to the window and saw the weather was being kind; just a few clouds—it was a beautiful sky. The smell of

Southern fried chicken was winding its way up the staircase already, and I knew that my mother was busy over the stove, crushing the Corn Flakes, breading the chicken and dipping it into oil to cook it for my picnic basket. That simple smell of cooking chicken so early in the morning I took as my mother's absolute approval of my date; but more important, she must be feeling good today. Deep down I knew she was romantic even though she didn't live her own life that way. Maybe that's why she got so excited about my romantic escapades. She had no objection to romance *as long as it wouldn't interfere with my career.*

"Good morning, Mom," I said, giving her a kiss as I came into the kitchen.

"Good morning, Brooke," she said, giving me a quick hug and snapping a pair of tongs like she was catching tsetse flies. "Were you able to sleep?" she asked with a twinkle.

"Yes," I said. "The chicken looks delicious."

"I'm making twelve pieces, just in case he's got a big appetite. If it's too much you can throw it overboard for the sea gulls."

"How do you feel this morning?" I asked, watching for what went unspoken.

"This morning I woke up feeling better than I have all week."

"Don't overdo it," I said, trying to take the tongs from her.

"No, I'm really enjoying it," she said, and I believed her.

My mother already had a lovely straw basket out

on the counter and an old red-checkered tablecloth that we never used except on evenings when my mother made a typically authentic American-Italian dinner, which meant spaghetti with Ragú sauce.

"I almost forgot napkins," she said as she ran to the hutch in the dining room and pulled out two red linen cloths.

"Wow, you're certainly making quite a picnic for us," I said, overwhelmed. "Thanks."

"I like doing it," she said. "I'm putting in two glasses, but you can buy the Coke later so it's cold."

"Okay, Mom."

"Now, I want you to use your head on this boat trip," my mother started more seriously. "Don't do anything foolish like jumping into the Sound because it looks good. There are sharks out there, and remember it's October and the water's got a chill to it already. I don't want you catching a cold."

"No jumping in the Sound."

"You're a smart girl, Brooke. I know you'll take care of yourself."

I took a spoon and started scooping out some of the fried Corn Flakes that never made it onto the chicken. The crunchy texture and zesty fried flavor gave the cereal a new dimension. As I was scraping around the sides of the hot pan for the last morsels, my thoughts drifted to Brandon.

"Do you think Brandon likes me a little?" I asked, searching for some assurance.

"He wouldn't ask you out if he hated you," she said, laughing.

"But I wonder in what way he likes me? As a friend? Or do you think he could like me more?"

"I think he likes you more."

"He smiles a lot at me and does try to sit next to me sometimes. During our last fire drill he touched the embroidery on the back of my shirt trying to figure out if it was a bird or a deer."

"Some boys are shy at first until they know the girl likes them. Boys like to play it safe, take the cue from the girl."

"What if I give the cue and he doesn't take it? I'd feel like an idiot."

"Be yourself, sweetheart. You like him, don't hide it. Don't play games. Don't jump on him, but don't play games. I know you see the difference."

Don't play games rang in my ears. Don't play games.

The drive to Brandon's country house was beautiful. My mother was still able to maneuver the car through traffic just like always. And as she drove she wasn't aware that I was staring at her. She really looked beautiful and springlike for this Indian summer day. Her nails were freshly done in a pink that picked up a touch of pink in her white-flowered dress. It reminded me of field upon field of anemones. I thought she had decided to wear it today because, as she had said when she bought it, "This is an 'up' dress. It reminds me of sunshine and makes me feel enthusiastic." That was her, all right. She was always enthusiastic. I was proud of the way she looked. Then I put my head toward the window to look at myself in the outside mirror to see if I looked as pretty as she did at that moment.

The directions Brandon's mother had given her the night before were very easy to follow.

"Here we are," my mother said, pulling up in front of a modest Cape Cod house.

I was relieved that it wasn't too big a home. Brandon saw us arrive and was at the front door before we could ring the bell.

"Hi, Brooke," he said, and he really looked happy to see me. "Hello, Mrs. Hillary," he said to my mother, making her feel very welcome. Brandon had his usual relaxed smile and there was something different about seeing him in this country setting. He seemed even more natural, more ordinary, not a rich-kid actor about to go out to Hollywood to be in a movie.

His home had modern furniture: a few chrome tables and a hanging lamp suspended from the middle of the room, a couple of leather sofas and beyond that some large glass windows leading onto a patio with white wrought-iron furniture. His mother came over immediately and warmly greeted us, putting my mother and me even more at ease. She appeared very sophisticated and worldly and gracious. As she walked toward us, I noticed a similarity between Brandon and his mother, especially around the eyes.

"Hello, Brooke," she said. "And *Claire*, how are you?" she asked my mother, extending her hand. "You're looking wonderful."

"Thank you," my mother said. "It was very lovely of you to invite me."

I must say that even though Brandon's mother knew about my Mom's illness, there was no trace of discomfort or awkwardness as they talked. I saw they would get along just fine. "Let's drop the kids off at the boat, then you and I can get ourselves a nice lobster salad at the club," Brandon's mother said, ushering us out to the car. Brandon's mother put her arm in my mother's and Brandon gave me a big wink as he picked up my picnic basket.

"Wow, what a lunch," he said, quite pleased. "It looks terrific."

"Thank you," I said, smiling to my mother, knowing that the compliment was certainly hers and not mine.

We waved good-bye to our mothers at the club and walked down to the main dock. There were hundreds of boats. Fishing boats, white yachts, little sailboats, some already rigged and heading out over the sparkling wave tips. "Most people don't like taking their boats out of the water," Brandon told me. "We hate to admit summer's over, but I'm afraid this will be my last ride of the season."

"What happens to your boat for the winter?" I wondered.

"It goes into hibernation; that's why this ride is so special and I thought you'd enjoy it."

I couldn't tell if he meant that romantically or maybe he just thought I liked water a whole lot, which I really don't. We passed people working on their boats as we made our way to the end of the pier.

"There she is," he said, proudly.

In front of us was a small fiberglass speedboat, and on it was painted the word *Apocalypse*.

"The *Apocalypse*?" I questioned.

"Yes," Brandon said, "my father gave it that name."

"What does it mean?" I asked.

"It's biblical—some kind of a big disaster."

"Sounds like the wrong name for a boat," I remarked.

"Yeah," he agreed, "I think it's the wrong name for anything."

He helped me into the boat and handed me the basket while he untied the mooring ropes from the pier. He got in, pushed us away from the dock and pulled the cord to start the outboard. The engine sputtered a few times, but then it roared. He moved some levers, then yelled, "Hold on," while the craft leaped forward.

When we were about a quarter of a mile from the shore, he said, "Here, you want to steer the boat?"

"Great," I cried out, never having done it before. A few sprays of water went in our faces and I was thankful I was wearing a red Windbreaker.

"You seem right at home on the high seas," he said.

"Thanks," I accepted. "I have to admit, though, I'm an earth person. I feel safer on land."

"I'm a water person for sure," he said. "In fact, that's my dream one day—I want to charter a large sailing ship and cross the Atlantic." He put his hand on top of mine to help me turn the engine slightly, and his touch was so wonderful I hoped he would never let go. The boat followed in an arc, and then he lifted his hand to point off to the right. "See that island over there? The one with the inlet and small beach?" I shielded my eyes and saw a stub of shining sand broken by clusters of wild plum trees and low green shrubs.

"Yes," I said.

"That's where we'll have our picnic. Right in the cove."

"Is that where you go to be alone?" I asked.

"Also when I'm happy." He grinned.

Within a few minutes he pushed the boat up on shore. I took off my shoes and we both walked around a few large rocks to get to the beach. Brandon put down a blanket, on which I placed the basket.

"Come on," he said, "let me show you around my island."

He took me by the hand and we ran through the sand until we reached a part of the beach covered with unusual shells. The tide had gone out and left a beautiful collection.

"Look," I said, "this one's perfect." I lifted a large conch shell. It was twisted, the kind you're supposed to put to your ear and listen to for the ocean.

"Listen," I said, as I put it to his ear. "I think this shell knows all your secrets."

He listened intently for a second. "Don't believe it." He shook his head. "This shell is bonkers."

We both burst into laughter again.

"Look at this one," he said, picking up a brown-

and-white shell and putting it to my ear. I closed my eyes and tried listening.

"This is my kind of conch," he said.

"Is it?" I asked.

"The sea talks," he replied.

"What does it say?"

"Can't figure that out." He laughed and I laughed with him. He held the shell out for me and I took it. My hand touched his for a moment and I slipped the shell into the picnic basket.

For hours we laughed and ran and felt free. We built a sand castle until the tide started to come forward and take it back. We brushed the drying sand from each other's backs. Then we picked some ripe red plums. The whole afternoon was going by too quickly.

"I'm famished," Brandon said.

"Chow's on," I yelled. "Last one back to the blanket is a wet fish." I lost the race, but I really didn't try to win. We ate almost all the chicken, as well as the potato chips. Brandon opened the bottles of Coke we'd picked up at the club and I offered him a choice between shortbread and chocolate chip cookies. We were so full that we just collapsed on the blanket. We didn't have enough energy to talk; we just looked straight up at the sun and closed our eyes, and we both fell asleep for a few moments. We were so quiet, it was as if we knew we didn't have to say a word to each other. I had never felt so close to another person in my life. He reached over and took my hand and then swung around, resting his head on my lap. I sat up, trying not to show how nervous and happy I was, but then I reached down and stroked his soft blond hair that fell into a few curls around his face. He closed his eyes and stretched and started to hum and moved my fingers to his lips. We listened to the waves breaking. Then, slowly, he reached both hands up and pulled me down to kiss him. We were together for hours but it seemed like minutes, and before I knew it I opened my eyes and saw him backlighted by streaks of yellow and purple tossed across the sky.

"Look," I said, "the sun is starting to set. Do you know what time it is?"

"I didn't bring a watch," Brandon said.

"I don't have one either, but I told my mother I'd be back by six."

"I can guess the time," Brandon said, "from the position of the sun. I'm sure it's past five-thirty."

"Maybe we should start back," I suggested.

"I suppose you're right," he said, kissing me again. Then we just looked at each other and I understood why some people can feel so happy they want to cry.

We threw everything onto the blanket and grabbed it so that it looked like we were carrying a dead man back to the boat. We swung it in, but before pushing the boat off Brandon stuck out his toe and wrote in the sand three large numbers, a 1, a 4 and a 3.

"One-four-three?" I inquired. "What does that mean?"

"It's a code. It means *I love you.*"

"How can one-four-three mean I love you?"

"It's the number of letters in each word."

I sat there silently figuring it out in my mind. "Oh" was all I could say. I didn't know whether he felt the way I did or was just telling me a mathematical equation. I wanted to believe that he was saying what I felt, too.

We stared into each other's eyes again. My heart soared like a bird finding its way home. I knew what it was to feel complete. *Don't play games.* It felt wonderful, I thought, then found myself whispering back, "One-four-three."

Brandon reached out and took my hand and smiled a smile I had never seen before, a smile that made me feel it was coming from a deeper place, beyond school, beyond Rudley's, beyond words. I felt his smile came right from his soul as though we had made a spiritual connection with each other. I had to break the intensity of the moment because it reached a new kind of pain for me—the one called happiness.

"I don't want my mother to worry about me," I said.

"Of course. I'm sorry," he said. We jumped into the boat and raced back out into the Sound. "The trip home is only about a half hour. Don't worry," he yelled over the roar of the motor.

"I won't," I said.

The water was calm and the sun was going down quickly. The yellows and purples of the sky were now darker, and clouds strung themselves along the horizon like sentries.

"Twilight is my favorite time of the day," I said.

"Why?" he asked.

"I feel it shows the world in its purest colors."

"I like dawn," he announced, "because I never know what it will bring."

It seemed as if almost half an hour had gone by, but I didn't see any land. It had gotten quite dark and the stars had come out.

"Brandon," I asked, over the noise of the pistons clanking and water churning, "did you take me out because you felt sorry for me?"

Brandon looked taken aback.

"I'm not a social worker," he said, looking right into my eyes.

"I'm sorry," I confessed. "It's hard for me to believe in anything good happening to me since I found out my mother was dying."

He shut off the motor and the boat began to drift. "I asked you out because I like you," he said, and I remembered 1-4-3 in the sand.

"I wanted to make sure," I said.

He reached out and took my hand. "You can be sure," he said firmly.

"I'm afraid, Brandon. Afraid of losing my mother. Afraid of being alone."

Brandon held me. "You won't be alone, Brooke."

"I'm afraid that anything I care about will die. I'm afraid of marriage and children. I'm afraid if I love my husband and children, they will die, too."

"Brooke, don't be afraid," he said putting his arm around me. "This is a hard time for you."

"Brandon, I have never seen anyone die. Have you?" He shook his head no.

"Are you afraid to die?" I asked him.

"No," he said. "I feel impervious to death. Sometimes I like speeding along an empty road at ninety miles per hour. Brooke, all of life is a gamble. It's that gamble that makes me feel alive. If I didn't take chances I'd be a big blob. Do you think it'll be easy for me to go out to Hollywood and face the cameras every day? I'm scared to death. But I'm going to do it. The picture might be awful. People might sit there and say that guy can't act for beans, but I'm going to gamble on it because I want big stakes in life. And so do you. Watch out," he said, standing up to start the engine again. He pulled the cord a few times and it wouldn't start. He pulled it again.

"What's wrong?" I asked.

"I'll have to let it rest a minute," he said. "I don't want to flood the engine."

After a few minutes, he pulled again and again and again on the cord. He stooped down, leaned over and pulled out the gas tank. I could tell from the way it rattled it was empty. He grabbed quickly for the reserve tank. We were stuck out there with two empty gas tanks!

"What will we do?" I asked, thinking of my mother worrying.

"Nothing—it'll be all right," he said. "Somebody must have taken this boat out and drained the reserve. They rip everything off nowadays. Sometimes they rip stuff off, then they bring it back."

"I'm not a good swimmer," I confessed. "I panic if my head goes underwater."

"How are you on the back float?"

"That's my best," I said.

"Look, don't worry, we'll sit here and wait for someone to pass by and give us a tow."

I looked around. By now it was getting dark and cold.

"A boat should be coming soon," Brandon said. "We're only a few minutes away. Don't worry, your mother won't be waiting long."

During the next fifteen minutes it got even colder, and the night air surrounded us as we drifted aimlessly into nowhere. Brandon was getting nervous but he took off his sweater and helped me slip it on. It was warm from him and I felt protected. Now it was so dark you could hardly see anything except the beacon from a lighthouse miles away. After what seemed like hours, we heard the sounds of a motorboat. Brandon and I both cupped our hands.

"Help, we're out of gas! Help! Help!"

"Do you think someone heard?" I asked.

"I can't tell," he said. "We'll see soon enough."

Then we didn't hear anything.

"Help! Help!" we screamed together again into the night. I could see my mother's face. She'd be very, very frightened.

Suddenly we heard the sound of a boat coming in our direction.

"One, two, three," Brandon directed, and we yelled together again. *"Help, this way, here we are!"*

A beam of light shot in our direction and a small fishing boat pulled up next to us. An old rugged-looking fisherman with whiskers stood up in his boat. "What are you kids doing out on the Sound at this hour?" he scolded.

"My motor's gone," Brandon said. "I'm out of gas!"

"You're kidding." He laughed. "Usually when a boy takes a girl out and runs out of gas, it's in a car and it's deliberate. Here, pull up," the fisherman ordered, "I'll give you a tow." The man threw a rope at Brandon, who tied it to the front of the boat and sat down next to me. "Hold on tight," he whispered. "We'll be home in a few minutes now. I'm sorry," he said, squeezing my hand. When we reached the dock, several people stood under a light. My mother was in the front and she looked drained. Brandon's mother was close beside her. Both of them talked so fast it all became one long run-on sentence. *We thought you got lost at sea we called the Coast Guard we called everybody what do you mean you ran out of gas what do you mean the motor conked out where were you what did you do Brooke you really scared me Brooke, why did you do that Brooke, you knew it was getting dark.*

"I'm sorry, I'm sorry," I kept repeating as someone wrapped a blanket around me and headed me toward a car. It was as though Brandon and I were being separated by all these people and our mothers talking so fast, *why this? why that?* But all I heard was a voice inside of me saying, *Hey, Brooke, what happened today is the most important thing in your life. What happened is more life-giving and exciting and electric than anything on any stage in the world.* I wanted Brandon's love more than anything in the universe. More than dancing, or applause, or anything! Maybe we were gambling for different stakes. He wanted success, but maybe he wanted the same stakes as I did when it came to us. *Yes,* I told myself. He does feel something for me. He does love me. I mean something to him and this time I have a chance. *This is what I want out of life,* I wanted to cry out. *This!* And without it I would die.

6

I knew I wouldn't see Brandon until lunch on Monday, and I kept looking at the clock. At twelve I walked into the lunchroom and Brandon rushed over. He grabbed my hand and pulled me to a table.

"Sit down a minute," he said with intensity.

"What's the matter?" I asked.

"Brooke, my agent called this morning. I have to be in California on Wednesday."

"So soon!" I said.

"I hate leaving because of you," he said, and I really believed he meant it.

I was happy for him, but here it was happening again. As soon as I cared for people, they left me. It was exactly the feeling I had tried to explain to him on the boat. Brandon wasn't dying, but now that I loved him he was going away—and to me that was a kind of death.

"You'll write, won't you?" Brandon asked.

"Of course I'll write," I answered.

"So will I," he said.

I touched his hand gently. We sat there without saying a word, looking at each other in the middle of a hundred kids banging trays and eating their sandwiches.

"I'm not good at saying good-bye," I said.

"I'll be back," he said.

"I know," I could barely say, because I wasn't certain of that at all. I just couldn't look at him, I was so sad. He moved close to me and put his arm around me. I had never had a boy do that in front of all the other kids before, but now I didn't care who was looking. It was just me and Brandon, and we couldn't speak. I put my head on his shoulder. Two teachers passing through the lunchroom looked at us but they didn't say anything. The bell rang and the lunchroom cleared and we still sat there while the kitchen staff cleaned up.

"I have to go now," Brandon finally said, putting his arms fully around me. I hugged him desperately, but then moved away embarrassed that I needed him so badly. He stood up. I looked up at him and smiled. He brought his hand to my cheek and I moved his fingers to my lips and kissed them. "Just a few weeks," he said. "I'll be back."

"Good-bye," I said. A part of me felt a surge of resentment that he was leaving just as we were beginning to trust each other. An invisible wall started to come up, shielding me from feeling too intensely again, from feeling too vulnerable. The risk of caring was simply too high.

November started off being the coldest month I can remember. It was getting dark too early now, and there were many days when the sun didn't shine at all. The squirrels were already collecting their winter rations in the park, claiming homes for themselves in the trees. I guess there are squatters' rights for squirrels, too. Sometimes I would bring some peanuts from home and sit on the bench in Central Park to feed them, watching them with their long bushy tails run up and down along the branches, stocking up for the winter. I felt like closing my eyes and shutting it all out, but time was too important. My mother seemed to be getting a little sicker. She had been to the doctor with my father the week before Thanksgiving. When I asked my father what the doctor said, he told me that some new medication for the pain had been ordered.

She found it harder and harder to eat. Even the Breyers maple walnut ice cream, which had been her downfall when she was dieting, was unappetizing. Her dresses hung loose as if they were a size too big. She tried to keep up her appearance of strength, but everything she did only showed how she was bluffing her way through each day, wanting to make us believe she was holding her own. It was then I noticed the pearl ring was not on her finger.

"Where's the pearl ring?" I asked, trying to be casual.

"It's in my drawer," she answered in the same tone. "It got too big for my finger. I would hate to see it go down with the dishwater." The whiteness of her skin, which had always contained a slight tinge of moisture—just enough to give it a glow—now seemed opaque; the muted skin tones replaced the glow that I remembered as if what plagued her from within could no longer be contained and was forced to move outward, toward the light. It was then that I recalled telling Brandon on the boat that my favorite time of day was twilight. Ironic as it may seem, at this very moment I felt my mother was facing the twilight of her life.

The day before Thanksgiving I heard my mother crying out in her sleep, "No. Don't do that! Stop. Don't do that again!" I jumped out of bed and ran to her, but my father already had the light on and was standing next to Mom, who seemed to be sleeping.

"Just a bad dream, Brooke dear," he said. "Go back to sleep."

I went back reluctantly, but her cries haunted me. Was her dream a memory from years ago, or a nightmare of what was to come?

Oh, Mom, I cried out to myself in bed, *hold back. We're not ready. Please, hold back.*

I began to think about how I would remember my mother after she was gone. One thing about my mother was that she always stuck by me and my brother—especially *me.* She had taught me what loyalty was. Pete and I knew we had one strong mother here, that we were always under her wing. But Pete wouldn't allow her to take over his life. Though Pete loved our mother he knew when to listen and when to stop listening. When to say, "Enough, Mom. Let me do it my way. It may not be the best way, but it's *my* way." I remembered the day his room was being redecorated and they were selecting colors. Mom had definite ideas that the room should be navy and maroon, but Pete insisted, "Brown." This discussion went on for days, but Pete's room is now brown. I remembered my mother trying to convince Pete that he shouldn't go out for a sport one season because of his low grades, but Pete made the soccer team and went to practice every afternoon until he had Mom coming to the game. My mother and father thought Pete had no direction because he followed his own voice. I was the one who didn't know what I was doing, because I only did what my mother told me. Playing the clarinet was a different story. My mother insisted Pete learn to play an instrument so Pete took clarinet lessons while I took piano lessons. Mom would make Pete go up to his room and practice, but then he'd proceed to sit on his bed and spend an hour inspecting the reed. Finally his clarinet lessons stopped when the teacher said Pete and the clarinet had not made a match. Pete never let my mother or father work him over, even though some evenings he would go to his room after another verbal disagreement and look beaten. But he wasn't. He was simply trying to decide his own life for himself.

As for myself, my mother made all the decisions.

She'd say, "Brooke, I made a dentist appointment for you on Friday at four P.M."

"Okay, Mom" was all I would say.

"Don't worry, honey, I'll walk you over and tell jokes while he drills," Mom would add. I never minded that she arranged everything for me because I knew no one would hurt me as long as she was around. She was a powerhouse. She was also the protector of the underdog; she'd fight hard for causes. With her being so wise and knowing, it was easy to let my mother plan the details of my day. I wanted to please her at all costs. Unlike Pete, who loved her as much as I did but was more relaxed about it.

After Thanksgiving Pete couldn't stand home anymore. Tension was building as my father began taking out more and more of his frustration on Pete. Pete agreed to go to agricultural school, and they were on trimesters so he would be able to leave right away. My father was pleased because he felt Pete was at last on some path toward a career.

The weekend before Pete was to leave for school brought a foot of snow, and we watched the flurries build to a blizzard. My father, Pete and I went out to start shoveling. Our fingers were freezing through wet gloves but in another way it was a warm time. We felt new closeness. On Sunday Pete and I went out in front of the frozen weeping willow tree and started building an igloo. After hours of stamping our feet, turning the snow into blocks of ice, we sat inside it and relished our palace of ice. I was glad Pete had been snowbound this weekend so we could play together the way we had when we were kids. Then my mother appeared in a woolen coat carrying two mugs. Her face looked drawn and thinner, and the starkness of the blazing snow accentuated the dark circles under her eyes, as if she hadn't had enough sleep. The loss of weight affected her smile by accentuating the bone structure in her face, which suddenly made her teeth seem larger than I had ever remembered.

"Thought the two of you would like some hot chocolate."

"Thanks," we both said as we took the steaming cups from her. I couldn't take my eyes off her face.

"Fine craftsmanship," she said, admiring our work.

"Won't you come in?" I said.

"I've got to get back to the kitchen. I'm making a meat loaf. See you kids later. Don't get too cold now," she said, turning away.

I watched her disappear into the side door.

"What are you thinking about?" Pete probed.

"About Mom," I answered. "Next winter she won't be here anymore," I said, looking at a thin crack in an ice block. "We'll have to make this winter last a long time."

"Brooke, she might not even make it to spring," he answered.

"But the doctor said she had a year," I said.

"A year at the most. Or it could just be a month. It could go very fast," he said.

"You know, we've never talked about what's happening," I said.

"I'm sorry," Pete said, "but I'm not able to—yet. I can't deal with it."

"Is that the only reason you're going away to school now?"

"Brooke, this is a horrible thing to say," he said slowly, "but I feel guilty. I hate that Mom is going to die. It rips me apart. It's something I can't face. I don't want to face. Do you mind?"

"No," I assured him. "I think I understand. At least I almost do," I added.

Monday morning arrived and Pete started out on his two-hour trek to school and said he'd drop me at the train. Mom saw us to the door with warnings to Pete about the treacherous roads and ice slips on the highway. Pete smiled back. "Don't worry," he said. On the way out I saw the sun starting to melt our igloo. Pete dropped me off at the train station and we waved good-bye to each other.

"If you need me, I'll be there" he said. And I knew he would be.

7

"Just a few weeks," Brandon had said, and here it was almost December and he hadn't come back. All I had were two postcards, one from the Beverly Hills Hotel on which he had scribbled, "Dear Brooke, I think of you every day. Tomorrow they're moving me to a hotel near Universal Pictures. I'll send you the address when I get it. *1-4-3*, Brandon," and a second card from Las Vegas on which all he wrote was "Wow" with an exclamation mark. The picture showed a chorus line of girls at the MGM Grand Hotel. I kept the cards under the seashell in my room. And I dreamed every night of Brandon coming back.

The audition for the *Lassie* program was postponed until the first week in December. What it ended up being was a big publicity gimmick where they were trying to bring attention to the program, whose ratings were not as high as had been expected. There were a lot of column items in the newspaper about what a difficult time the producers were having in finding a costar for a *Lassie* segment. And there were all sorts of shots of Lassie at Rockefeller Center, Lassie at Radio City Music Hall and even Lassie riding a Fifth Avenue bus.

"I was thinking last night," my mother said, her voice thinner, weaker, reminding me that her illness was beginning to drain her, "that maybe you should do that tap dance you do in your toe shoes. That would surely get the producer's attention."

"Ma," I said, "toe tapping while jumping rope to 'There's No Business Like Show Business' is not what *Lassie* needs." But then I caught myself. My tone was wrong. My voice sounded too angry. "I think that wouldn't be right, maybe," I said quickly.

"Maybe you're right," my mother agreed, knowing I was thinking of her sickness. "Something a little more conservative might be called for. You'd better just do your *Slaughter*. You got very far in the Police Athletic Competitions with that. Oh, Brooke"—she beamed enthusiastically—"wouldn't it be wonderful if you got the part? It would be your big chance." She made it all sound so urgent, so important it scared me. It was as though Nature had placed a time bomb in the house and I would have to hurry before it exploded.

We were talking at the dinner table, which was where my mother and father usually did discuss my fate, right in front of me. My father was listening all along. "Let's not build up her hopes in case she doesn't win," he said. "We don't want her to be disappointed." He sounded more gentle than usual.

"One of these auditions she's going to get. I know it," my mother said.

"Yes, Claire," my father agreed. I knew he didn't want to upset her.

"I happen to think the only way you achieve anything in this world," my mother said, her voice straining, "is if you set your goals for exactly what you want, nothing less. That's the only way you get anyplace." She turned to me. She looked uncomfortable, as though she was fighting physical pain. "What's the episode called?"

" 'Lassie Loves New York,' " I said.

"Right," my mother was reminded. "Brooke would play a girl who communicates with Lassie through dancing in order to rescue a little boy lost in Central Park. It's a perfect part for her, and I'm sorry you don't think so."

"I didn't say that, honey," my father said.

"If you only had more drive," my mother said, angry that there was no one at the table quite as convinced of my chances of success as she was, "you would have been a doctor like you wanted instead of an accountant."

Now that was true, my father had always wanted to be a doctor, but unfortunately his father (my grandfather) got cataracts and couldn't work, so my father had to drop out of medical school to work and support his seven younger sisters and brothers. That was a great sacrifice for my father to make, I knew, but my mother saw it as a failure. Perhaps the fact that my father had to switch his goals from what he wanted made him more protective of my feelings. By playing up the academic part, he encouraged me to go to college just in case my theatrical career didn't get off the ground. Yet at the same time he'd be the first person applauding in the audience, saying to the stranger sitting next to him, "That's my daughter." He was definitely proud of me, but he wanted me to be realistic about my chances, and he knew that life can throw some curves like the one that hit my mother at Brighton Beach and changed his life.

"Brooke," my mother said, "you've got to try *harder*."

"Yes, Mom," I agreed, and I heard the ticking of a bomb again, but I suppose it had always been there.

Mom's philosophy was symbolized in that pearl ring she had always worn. And when her mother gave it to her, she instructed Mom that the pearl stood for *freedom*. "Whenever I look at this pearl I remember what my mother taught me," my mom once told me, "and I want to teach you the same thing. Remember, Brooke, just remember—you can be anything! You can be a doctor or a lawyer or an astrophysicist—the world is your oyster." That was one thing good about our house, I always felt it didn't matter whether I was a boy or a girl, I could do anything in the world I wanted, even be president. I wasn't taught that being a female was a handicap. I was always told the world was as good for me as it was for a man. Once I asked my mother, "What if I want to be a housewife? Is there something wrong with that?" I remember my mother being a little taken back.

"If that would make you happy, Brooke," she had responded slowly. "I do know lots of women who are perfectly happy being housewives, but I don't think you will be. You were meant for greater things," she said.

"Isn't being a housewife and a mother a great thing to be?" I asked.

"I hate the word *house* wife. I'm not married to the house," my mother insisted. "I'm not *its* wife. It sounds archaic, *old-fashioned.* I love my children and my work, honey. But we are living in different times; you can have all that and more. *You* can have all the things that I couldn't."

"Would you be very disappointed in me if I wanted to be a terrific houseperson like you?" I pursued.

"Oh," she said, suspiciously. "You're not still daydreaming about Brandon, are you? I've seen those postcards since he left for Hollywood. Don't let him stand in the way of your career, because if you did that, Brooke, let me tell you you'd be making a big mistake. He wouldn't let you stand in the way of his."

"Can't I have a family and a career?" I asked.

"Brooke, you have to have meaning in your life, not just go hitchhiking in any direction you wish. You need a vision of something higher than just what you'll be doing next Saturday."

"While I lose my chance of someone to really love me?"

"A family will come in due time. First you must think of making a place for yourself. That's what your job is right now. Don't you understand, Brooke, making something of yourself? Otherwise you'll be a dilettante. Dabble here and there. Draw a little. Paint a little. Dance a little. And do none of these things well. Do you want to be that, Brooke? Do you? A dilettante?"

"No, Mom, but . . ."

"But what?" she asked me.

I was afraid to reveal my inner feelings because I knew it would get my mother angry. "Nothing," I said.

"But what, Brooke?" she pursued, wanting to understand my conflict.

"But what if I achieve all that at the expense of losing Brandon?"

"My God. You can't go around planning your life around Brandon."

"Why not?"

"Is he planning his life around you?"

"No."

"You see. He's not thinking about love and romance. He's in Hollywood making a picture."

"I guess, Mom, what I'm trying to say is that maybe I want something simpler than all that glitter."

"What do you want?" she asked bluntly.

"I want to care about someone and have someone care about me."

"You're filled with idealistic passion and you should be at your age. But that's where we come in, Dad and I, to give you some direction so you don't become a misguided missile."

"Yes, Mom," I said, trying to end the discussion

because I could tell I was getting her angry, which I didn't want to do.

"And let me tell you another thing: When you get older you'll find out that a man doesn't want a woman totally dependent on him. It's a real drain. He wants an independent woman who can do her own thing. Be an independent person in your own right, get out in that world and do something that *you* want. Something that excites you. Something that wins your own respect and is self-fulfilling. You come first. You have to be your own person, and carve out a niche for yourself. Then and only then, after you have found yourself, will everything fall into place. You'll get everything you want. But don't do it for Brandon or any man. You must do it for yourself. Don't look for a man to fulfill your own dreams and fantasies. He shouldn't be your meal ticket or an excuse to leave home, or anything like that. Don't look for someone to achieve the very things that you should be achieving. Have the courage to know what you want and act on it. Then you can have a really healthy, enriching relationship. Then you will be a good wife and mother. You won't feel you've missed the boat. Believe me, honey, I want all that for you. But first you must realize your potential. I want you to know that you have *choices* in life. It's those choices that give you freedom to be. It's my job as your mother to teach you that. It's my job because I love you," she said, letting out a deep sigh as if she had poured out her soul.

Out the kitchen window the wind was tossing the branches of the peach tree and Russian olive tree, the thin branches of the Russian olive caressing the heavier branches of the stronger peach tree. The cool wind filled me with an urge to run out the door and away from this discussion.

"Brooke," my mother said, "I can't just stand by and watch you throw away all those classes, all those things you worked for. All those years of preparation."

I just stared out the window.

"Is it wrong to want you to have more than I had?" she asked me, trying to explain the feelings to herself. Her thumb was playing with a wrinkle in her skirt as if it was a hot iron trying to get a crease out.

The last thing I wanted to do was upset her, but it made me wonder if I was alone in my feelings. Were there other kids out there whose parents wanted them to be big school football heroes, or presidents of the class? The pressure to succeed must be felt by a lot of kids I know. To live up to our parents' expectations of us, to make them proud of us, to love us. What price do we pay for their love? Maybe they know things we don't. . . . Maybe we do need direction, but I feel that if I ever had any kids of my own, I would let them have the freedom to be whatever they wanted. I thought back about the pearl ring. And my grandmother's instructions to my mother. The pearl stood for freedom. What if that freedom was passed on to me? What would I do if I got it?

I knew one thing, that I had to reconcile my feelings for a career and the burning need to be loved. Could I successfully combine them both? If I didn't, I would surely lose out in both directions.

She came over and put her arm around me and I smelled the lemon fragrance which she sprayed on in the morning.

"Aim high, honey. Aim for the stars," she said, adding her favorite line: "People look for Mars and Jupiter in the skies, but inside of us is where we find our own dreams."

"Mom, can't I just aim for something a little closer? I'm only sixteen."

"You won't be sixteen forever. Know what you want and work for it! Don't you understand, honey? You've got to do it now!"

I became frightened as I realized what she was telling me. I began to realize my mother desperately wanted me to become famous before she died. I didn't know how much longer she had to live—maybe six months, maybe less. There was no way I was going to be a star by then, no matter what I did. But I saw too that she had convinced herself that it was I who wanted to be a star.

"What about Pete?" I asked, changing the subject. "What about his career?" My mother looked away. "We're doing the best we can for Pete. He's floundering a little but seems to be finding himself. I'm glad he decided to go to school. It's the best thing for him," she said.

"Do you know what Pete told me?" I had to say. "Last week they made him kill a chicken and he ran to the bathroom and threw up. The instructor came after him and told him he had to do it to get credit for the course and Pete answered back, *I'm no chicken killer*. Do you think he'll stick it out?" I asked, though I knew Pete wouldn't do anything he didn't want to.

"Suppose we just worry about you," my mother suggested. It was then that I thought, there might be a price too great for someone's love.

The day of the *Lassie* audition arrived and my mother came into Manhattan to meet me after school and go to the studio with me on Forty-seventh Street. She was carrying a Bloomingdale's shopping bag with my costume and a tape of *Slaughter on Tenth Avenue.* "Are you nervous?" she asked.

"Very," I confessed.

"You're getting jitters, stage fright. That's very normal. I read somewhere that a world-famous cellist once went and hid under a table before he had to play a concert and he had been in the business over thirty years. You simply have to learn to cope with stage fright in this business. Use it. It will make you give a better performance," she instructed.

"What if they don't like me?" I said, rejected already.

"Of course they'll like you, honey. You just relax and you'll win them over. Remember to really go for the elevation when you do those flip-flops at the end."

"I will, Mom," I said.

She was so excited, it was hard to believe she was so sick!

We opened the door to the studio and gave my name to the girl at the reception desk. She checked my name off a long list and we were shown into a large room.

"You can change in here," one of the assistants told me, "then wait for your name to be called."

"I'll meet you back here," my mother told me. "I'll try to see what the competition is."

I changed real fast. I was getting very, *very* nervous. When I had finished getting into the somewhat dazzling sequined costume my mother had made me, I joined her and the other kids and mothers in the main waiting room. I saw two girls from my school. One was Rosalind Urbell, a girl I had never particularly liked. She was very snooty and acted as though she was already a star. She was dressed in a purple costume with fringe that was even louder than mine. The other girl was someone whose name I couldn't remember, but she was in my biology class. I thought she was too heavy to be a dancer. I thought she might be something like a teenage comedienne or have a talent for playing the piano. All the mothers and kids were trying to look very cool and collected as they waited, but the tension was enough to ignite a hydrogen bomb. I decided the only way I could get through it was to think of Brandon. Wouldn't he be thrilled if I got the part he had told me about that first night he called? And then I remembered him reaching toward me, bringing me to him for our first kiss on his secret island. He would come back soon. He *had* to.

I had already crossed off eight weeks on my calendar. That meant three weeks to Christmas, when I just felt he'd be home. What could I do to make three weeks go by fast? I could keep busy every minute. Take a lot of classes, shop for some clothes and get my hair trimmed. Then I would be ready at any moment for Brandon to come home and surprise me. Surely he'd be home for Christmas. I felt like something new and crisp. Maybe cut my hair shorter. Get rid of the bangs I had had since I was born. Maybe I wasn't ready to get rid of those, but . . .

The increased nervous chatter brought me back to reality. I licked my lips to make them glisten.

A man started walking past me toward the tape recorder with a pile of tapes. The producers were sitting right in front of a stage area and there were several men in a sound booth; there was also a photographer taking a lot of pictures, which was unusual for any ordinary audition. Some of the girls *sang* and danced; many just danced. Three girls had picked exactly the same audition song, and one girl did an elaborate mime to "I Enjoy Being a Girl." I wondered how so many girls had shown up and where all those mothers had come from. Why did everybody want to get into show business? Was it always someone's mother or father who had caught the bug and passed it on to their kids? I kept watching Rosalind Urbell and she did nothing but play with her fringe, which made me even more nervous. When Rosalind did her routine, it seemed to consist of nothing but twirling—she kept spinning around and kicking out her legs to the tune of "Hey, Look Me Over."

Finally, I heard my name called. Actually, it was

my mother who heard it called and tapped me on my arm. I was still dreaming of Brandon, of his head on my lap, stretching, humming as I smoothed his beautiful hair.

"It's you," she said.

"Oh, God" was all I could muster.

"Good luck," my mother whispered.

As I started running up toward the stage area, I forgot how my dance began. As a matter of fact, I forgot all the steps. My hands had gotten ice cold. My heart was jumping a mile a minute and I wanted to run out of the room!

Have courage, I started saying to myself. Have courage.

I made it to the stage and looked around. To me, the stage always became a test and I was terrified of failing. I didn't want to disappoint my mother and I wanted the producers to like me.

Then there was silence. I looked out at the people in the room. I could hear my mother whispering, "Gather yourself," and so I closed my eyes for a fraction of a second to find the center of me, as she would say. I could hear her voice, "Find the center, the center." The music started and after the first moment, it all came back to me. I stopped thinking and just let my body take over, one step leading to the next, just as I had rehearsed it over and over again the last few months. Then as the music builds in *Slaughter*, I became aware I was halfway through. It was almost over and I'd be finished. I couldn't forget about all the people sitting out there, about all the judging, about

Rosalind Urbell's fringes and my mother and father. I couldn't wait for the last ten bars; then before I knew it the music built to a crescendo and I landed in a split. Four minutes of dancing felt like an hour onstage, and was I relieved that it was over. The audience applauded and I smiled. I went back to my seat knowing that I had done the best I could. My mother seemed pleased, too, which made me feel wonderful.

Now we just had to wait until the end, when the judges would announce the winner. That was the hardest part of all, the part I couldn't prepare for.

There were seven more girls after me and then the producers got into a huddle in the corner for several minutes of consultation. Finally a distinguished-looking man got up on the stage and everyone sat absolutely still. This producer said that this had been a promotional audition to arouse local interest in the show. Then he went on about being very pleased and appreciative of all the fabulous participation by the young people and all the support from their parents. "However," he said, "the difficult part has been selecting the winner."

All I wanted was for someone to let me out of this suspense, and a glass of water because my throat was dry. The next moment could make the difference between anonymity and a new streak of fortune. Looking over to my mother, I could see the hopeful anticipation in her eyes as she sat forward in her seat waiting for my name to ring out in the auditorium. A part of me was afraid to wish I had won. I had danced the best

I could. The question was: Had they picked me as winner?

"With much difficulty and deliberation," the producer continued in a very professional-sounding monotone, "we have selected a young girl who has a great deal of charm and talent."

I'm sure every one of the girls thought it was herself.

"This girl shows signs of being a great performer. The winner is . . ."

There was complete silence.

". . . Rosalind Urbell," he said with great animation.

"Rosalind Urbell," I said to myself, incredulously. It wasn't my name he said. It wasn't *me*. I sat there dumbfounded a moment, trying to digest the news. I think this is what you call shock. All I said to myself was *Don't cry. Don't let my eyes give away the disappointment and rejection I am feeling at this moment.* To do this, I kept my eyes focused on an empty spool of tape. That helped hold back the tears. Then I exhaled and felt a tremendous relief. Win or lose, the months of pressure that had built up were over. Tonight I could go to sleep without worrying whether I'd win the audition or not. Now I knew.

Various sounds broke out in the room, from astonishment to hushed disagreement, as everyone hid her disappointment and applauded the winner. Rosalind went up onstage to receive her congratulations from the producers.

"Don't worry about it—you can't win them all," my mother said consolingly. "We'll just move on to the next one."

"Right, Mom," I said, grabbing my Bloomingdale's shopping bag and starting up to the dressing room to change out of my costume. "I'm sorry."

"Don't worry," Mom said. "The next one, that'll be the big one."

As I went off, I looked back. My mother had burst into tears and she was openly crying, her arm covering her eyes. She never knew I had seen her. I remember feeling that this particular audition I had lost to Death.

As I was walking back toward the dressing room, there was Lassie standing in the wings. This wasn't the original Lassie, because that one died a long time ago, but this was the Lassie which was the "Lassie of today" and I bent down and petted him and tickled his stomach. He reached over and licked my face. Then he gave me his paw and I shook it.

"Hi, Lassie," I said and petted him again. And everything seemed better. Maybe I hadn't won—and my mother was terribly disappointed—but I was happy that I had shaken hands with Lassie. That was the best part of the whole thing. Prizes can come in all sorts of shapes and colors and sizes, and some of them *bark*. Winning wasn't the answer. What was important to me was contact with someone, even if that someone happened to be a dog. What was important was someone accepting me for what I was. I reached out and the dog responded to *me*, *Brooke Hillary*.

Feelings, I said. *Feelings. That's what I want above all.*

Brandon wouldn't be disappointed in me. He would be there when I needed him. He would put his arm around me and remind me of all that life could be. Should be. He would be home for Christmas, I was certain. Any day there would be a letter and soon he would touch and kiss and hold me again.

8

The week before Christmas my mother was at the stores as they opened in the morning to complete the Christmas shopping she had been doing slowly over the last few months. She really rallied and got in the spirit of Christmas, especially when she received her money from the Christmas Club and some extra money my father had given her. He wanted her to buy whatever she wanted, and we all knew this Christmas had to have real magic. I was trying hard to think of something to give her, something she had always wanted. Then it came to me. A cheery caftan, something she'd be comfortable in if someone came to visit, and I remembered how she loved to wear happy colors for us because once when I was ten, she overheard some of my friends saying how they loved that my mother always dressed in "happy-looking clothes." And that she smelled good, too.

A few days before Christmas my mother and I went out to buy a tree. We found a seven-foot spruce that we both fell in love with and had it delivered to our house. That evening my mother, father, Pete and I started unwrapping the ornaments we had collected over the years. My father set up the lights. Pete got on a stepladder and started hanging some of the ornaments as we passed them up, sometimes giving directions as to what branch. I could tell this was an intense time for my mother. She would unwrap some of the old Christmas decorations that Pete and I had made when we were kids. Some of the paper had turned brown and the original sparkles had fallen off, but she held each one as if it was a delicate pressed flower. "Remember when you made this papier-mâché candle, Brooke? You said you were going to leave this next to the door for Santa since we didn't have a fireplace, and you also wanted to give him one of your favorite toys. That year it was your doll, Erica."

"That was silly, wasn't it?" I said, giggling.

"No, it was a nice thought," she answered.

"When I woke up in the morning, the first thing I'd check before opening my presents was if Santa took my present. The toys were always gone. What did you do with them each year?" I asked her.

"After you went to bed, I'd put it up in the attic. Then, inevitably a few weeks later, you'd miss your favorite toy and lo and behold, one of your older cousins just happened to be giving the exact toy away. And I'd bring it down from the attic."

"I never really believed your Santa stories," Pete said devilishly.

"Never?" I asked incredulously. "You always acted like you did."

"Not since I was four and I woke up very early for my Christmas presents, so early that Mom and Dad hadn't gone to bed yet, and they were busy running back and forth to the closet pulling out all our presents," Pete explained.

"I didn't know that," my mother said, taken aback.

"Don't worry, Mom. You didn't ruin the surprise. I already knew what I was getting anyway because I knew all your best hiding spots." We all laughed.

"How do you like your presents this year?" she asked, and Pete laughed.

"I'll hang this," my mother said, holding up a green shiny musical bell with a tassel that she had bought as the new ornament for this year.

"There," she said, finding just the right branch.

Everything was in place—the lights, the ornaments, the bird on top. "Lights out," Pete said, turning off the lights. My mother went over to the tree and wound up the bell, and we all stood entranced at the magic as "Silent Night" rang out from it. We stood there together, gazing at the tiny twinkling lights. Then Mom kissed me and I kissed her, then I kissed my father and my brother came over and kissed me and Pete went over and put his arms around my father and gave him a big hug. Somehow whatever was happening between us, working together, the tree, the magic, I don't know exactly, but it brought us together as a family, and the closeness I felt as we hummed

"Silent Night" to the sound of the musical bell became permanently captured in my mind, making me want to recreate this moment again and again. Someday I would with my own family and with my own children. My father looked lovingly at my mother and Pete and me. There are times when having a family is great.

As lovely as holidays are, though, they can accentuate loneliness—*that* I really found out.

Brandon had left close to three months ago and it seemed years. I knew he would write to say when he'd be coming home. I knew he knew I was constantly thinking about him and he'd probably want me to meet him at the airport. Or would he surprise me? No. He would write. But one thing I felt sure of—that he'd be home by Christmas.

I was feeling bad. My throat hurt a great deal. The only time I had been out of the house in the last few days was when my mother took me to the doctor. After examining me, he had asked me to leave the room, which made me suspicious. One word I did pick up was *hypochondriacal*. I knew it meant my sore throat was supposed to be in my mind. Now that's quite a trick, to have a sore throat of the mind, but that's what the doctor told my mother I had.

My mother walked out of the doctor's office and smiled at me, not knowing I had had my ear to the door. "Well, honey," she had said, "it's nothing that a few days' rest and some Tender Loving Care won't cure. And he's given me some pills for you."

Ha, I thought, *sugar pills, that's what they are*.

"You have to take one four times a day," she said.

"Sure," I agreed, deciding I'd better just play along with it. My mother put her arm around me supportively as we walked to the car. At least I thought at first it was to hold me up, but then I realized she was actually beginning to lean on me. Her illness was truly beginning to take its toll, and I felt terrified.

"I think this is a hard time for you, honey," my mother said, embarrassed that she needed my support.

"Oh, Mom, don't feel sorry for me," I said irritably. "I just have a sore throat." Then I felt a surge of love and admiration for my mother. How she could hold back all her feelings from me so I wouldn't worry any more than I did. No wonder I loved and respected her so much, because she was capable of finding courage at a time like this. The last thing she wanted was pity. Then I thought what it would be like when she was dead. Where would she go? Would she die and that's the end, nothing more? Or is there really a heaven? Would her spirit fly around waiting to be reborn in a yet unconceived child someday? Maybe in me? I couldn't think of her not talking and breathing and laughing with me. Not filling the house. What if I wanted to ask her what she thought about Nancy and me going to Europe next summer? Or what we should do next Friday night? Or call her up on the phone to tell her I'd be a few minutes late, only she would never speak to me on the other end. What would it be like not having a mother anymore? At that moment I wanted to scream out, *You will live forever, because as long as I'm living and breathing, you will live. We are intertwined, you and I, my eyes are your eyes, they have been colored by you, and somehow your energy is seeded deep within me.* I remembered reading something by Jean-Paul Sartre, the French philosopher, who said that a person lives as long as they remain in your thoughts, and dies when you no longer think about them. I knew my mother would live every day of my life. I wanted to tell her, "Mom, I will make you immortal. You will live forever through me, through my children and my children's children."

Mom must have sensed my inner scream.

"I know it's hard on you. I'm sorry," my mother said, putting her arm around me. I wanted to hold on to that moment, because as much as I hated facing it, I knew that someday soon her touch, her voice, this moment would be memories.

Two days before Christmas, I was still in bed. I was trying to work on a paper due when I got back to school, when I heard the mailman open the letterbox. Somehow I knew there would be a letter for me. The letter would make up for everything, it would explain how busy he had been, that he couldn't write until he could tell me that he was going to see me again. This would be the last letter before I saw him. *Before I saw him!*

There was a letter addressed to me. There was no return address on the outside, but the postmark said California and I recognized the handwriting. I ran up to my room and jumped back into bed, because I wanted to savor each and every word. I tore the letter open and read it slowly.

"Dear Brooke," it said,

I am writing this letter from the American Airlines counter at Los Angeles airport. I'm going on location in Juneau, Alaska. I just had to let you know I was thinking of you and I'm so sorry that I'm not going to be able to see you during the holidays. My mother called me at the Sportsman's Lodge where I was staying while I was at Universal, and she told me that the producers of the film had called her and they needed to do some snow scene exteriors in Alaska. They said my part would be getting bigger because they wrote out the other kid's part (he wanted more money) and so they're rearranging the shooting schedule. I tried calling you between packing and leaving the hotel, but the line was busy and I finally had to go. I am sorry that I will not be able to see you under the mistletoe, but remember *1-4-3*.

Signed, "Brandon."

At the bottom of the letter was an address where he would be staying in Alaska. I read the letter again and again. I read it so many times that morning I almost wore out the paper. I felt elated that he had written 1-4-3 to me, but the news that I would not be seeing him for Christmas made me crash.

I felt like talking to my mother, but she wasn't back from shopping. Finally, I decided the only way I could stop my pain was to answer his letter. I took a pen from my desk and put it in my mouth as I searched frantically for just the right piece of stationery to use. I kept a box with interesting cards that I had collected over the years from museums and stores and nostalgia shops. I finally selected a piece of silver paper with a silkscreen of a unicorn on the envelope. I knew he would like that. At least I knew he sure as heck would notice it. I curled up on my bed and started writing.

Dear Brandon, I don't know how I'm going to be able to make it to school in January knowing you won't be there. Just going will seem so empty because there won't be anyone in the classroom without you—no matter how many kids there really are. I miss your smile so much. You don't know what an important person you've become in my life. The memory of our day in the boat and at your private cove is the only thing I have to try to forget my loneliness. You are my one joy at this time of my life. I get up in the morning for you, I dress for you, I live just to see you. You make me feel alive and I pray each night that you want to be with me as much as I want to be with you. Your presence is with me in everything I do. Please forgive me if I skip the numbers and just come out with it. Brandon, I love you very much. I love you so much I don't care if the rest of the world knows. If you want me to leave school, if you want me to run away, if you need me in Alaska, just say the word, I'll be there somehow, some way. There was a Chinese saying on love I wanted to share with you. "If you want to know how much it is I love you, go to Tago Bay and count the waves rolling into shore." Oh God, Brandon, please love me as much as I love you. All my love forever and ever, Brooke.

That was the letter I really wanted to send him. I reread it twice and decided to tear it up. I felt too hurt he wasn't coming home. In spite of his signing 1-4-3 I felt totally rejected. My desperation had shown in the letter. He mustn't see that, I thought. I would write something else. I would play a game. *Don't play games,* my mother had warned, but I had to protect myself against this hurt. What I wrote and sent him was this:

Dear Brandon, I was surprised to hear from you and I'm thrilled about your new movie. I'll bet Juneau is absolutely beautiful with all the snow and icicles hanging from the trees. You're such a good actor I know all your movies are going to be successful.

Your mother must be awfully proud of you. We all are. We all know you're going to be the next John Travolta. I didn't get the part in the *Lassie* show, but I just bought the new issue of *Show Business* and I'm lying in bed addressing envelopes to a whole list of agents and producers, a lot of whom have shown interest in my work. I have a very busy month planned. School seems awfully quiet without you. There's no one to make us laugh in biology class anymore. All the kids miss you, especially me. Please write me and let me know how all those Hollywood stars are treating you and what you're thinking.

I hesitated and then signed, "1-4-3. Yours sincerely, Brooke."

When my mother finally did come home, she looked dangerously exhausted but I couldn't stop myself from telling her about the letter, that Brandon had actually thought of me at the American Airlines counter in Los Angeles airport.

"Well, don't be too disappointed, Brooke," she said. "You knew he was on his way up."

"But he cares for me," I said, looking for some reassurance from her.

"Sure he cares for you, honey," Mom said, "but just remember, he cares for his career most of all. Any real star loves his career first, Brooke, and I want you to remember that. Brooke, do you remember the time you were nine years old and were playing blind man's buff across the street, you closed your eyes and your friends hid and they were supposed to tell you when you were getting hot or cold? Well, all your friends you trusted to steer you in the right direction disappeared and you walked smack into a brick wall. Do you remember we rushed you to the doctor and you needed four stitches? Do you remember what you said to me after?"

"Yes," I said, softly.

"Yes. You said, 'I'm never going to walk into a brick wall with my eyes closed again.' That's what you said."

"I remember," I said.

"Good," she said. "Oh, Brooke." She sighed, hiding her few presents in the hall closet. "If only someone would give you a break soon," she added, and I knew what that meant.

9

During Christmas vacation when Pete was home from agricultural college, he was shocked to see the changes in my mother. She was much weaker, and had lost about fifteen pounds since he had left for school. She was frailer, more vulnerable. Usually before Pete my mother would put up a front, but now she didn't have the energy. I suppose Pete saw for the first time, after having been away so long, the effects the illness was having on her. He spent a lot of time in his room or running out for pizza. Occasionally my mother asked Pete to stay a few minutes and talk to her. When he came out of her room, he was white as a ghost. I always wondered what they talked about. He would just walk out of the room, get into his car, drive away and come back drunk a few hours later. Sometimes I'd wake up in the middle of the night and find him passed out somewhere between the living room and the up-stairs landing.

Then before I knew it, vacation was over. Pete went back to school.

"Can I come with you?" I asked him half seriously.

"Sure," he said, opening the car door, "hop in." I was tempted. I didn't want to see my mother wearing away, changing, becoming more like a child. I didn't want to see my father help her up the stairs every night, each step like a mile. I didn't want to pass her bedroom when she was asleep and think this is how she'll be for all eternity. A part of me wanted to run away too, leave my mother before she left me, but I knew I could never desert her even though she was leaving me in another way.

"Brooke," I heard my mother's voice calling from the kitchen. "Come in. You don't have a jacket on."

I watched Pete back out of the driveway, and I waved good-bye and kept waving good-bye until he turned the corner onto Dutch Broadway, then when I couldn't see the black top of his car any longer ran back into the house.

"He's on his way back to those chickens," I said, trying to cover my disappointment that he was gone. She smiled, maybe sensing my feeling of desertion.

I was trudging through the snow in the middle of January, going to classes and a lot of auditions. I got every show business paper I could get my hands on, I read every bulletin board I could find. I cut a lot of classes to make every audition, every photo and resume submission, I could possibly dig up. January is a depressing month anyway; spring seems so far away, the spring that I didn't want to come. There was no time to hibernate now. I was busy storing up moments while my mother was here. . . . Her life wasn't running according to a calendar year. It was on a different rhythm. Some nights I would hear her crying in her room. I felt helpless about her—and my father—and even Pete. I was not sure at all that he wanted to go to that college. And I missed the Pete-who-used-to-be when we were growing up. I always did things for him, but I loved doing them. If he wanted a carton of chocolate ice cream, I would go right down to the store and get it. I just liked making him happy, like I wanted to make my mother happy, and I was proud that he was my brother and friend, and even though I was his kid sister I know he liked me, too. If only Brandon had been home—I could have talked to him about it all.

The twenty-third job I went for in January was as a model to do a liquor commercial, but they asked me my age and when they found out I was a minor they asked me politely to leave. The next audition after that one was on Broadway and Forty-eighth Street. They were looking for a girl who was between eighteen and twenty, so I put on my most sophisticated dress and piled my long black hair up to make me look older. This was an understudy part for an off-Broadway production. They took one look at me and said they needed a blonde. I went to an open call for the chorus of a new Broadway musical. It was set in the sixties, so I pulled my hair straight down and tried to create the sixties look with what I was wearing. Everyone knows that an open audition is called a "cattle call," and that is a very good name. About a hundred people are shown into one large room at a time and given a card with a number, then you fill out the back with all your credentials, name, address, telephone. The room was swamped with people of all shapes and sizes and many were dressed in strange outfits. I was the youngest one there, except maybe for one boy with long red hair who was wearing a vest and pants made out of soda-bottle tops.

Two hundred fifty-four, that was my number and I was being called. I marched with nine others into a huge mirrored room with a piano. Then the producer's assistant asked us to stand there and hold up our numbers. The producer sat on a chair in the middle and studied us all for a few seconds, then he pointed to a girl and a boy in the line and said, "Two hundred forty-nine and two hundred fifty-three, please stay. The others, thank you very much," he said. *Imagine.* "Thank you very much." That's all he said after we waited on line for two hours, all he said was "Thank you very much."

I went to the bottom floor of the building to a newspaper stand and bought a chocolate bar. I was munching away when the boy in the soda-bottle-top outfit came in to buy a pack of Trident gum. "I guess you didn't make it either," he said, jingling.

"Nope," I answered. "That's why I'm eating candy," I informed him.

"Well, you gotta have a gimmick," he said, "something that makes you stand out in a crowd."

"Is that why you wear that outfit?" I asked, without any judgment in my voice.

"Yeah," he said, "they call me Top Pop, and when I'm not working I make dolls and trucks out of soda-bottle tops. Say, who's your agent?" he inquired.

"I don't have one," I confessed.

"Oh, girl, you've gotta get yourself one," he insisted. "That gives you clout." He took a piece of paper and started writing. "Here's my agent's number. He's not a crook. Just tell him I said you should call." And then he gave me a wink and turned and zipped into a crowd of people rushing through the lobby.

I yelled, "Good luck at your next open call," but I don't know whether he heard me or not. I remembered Brandon had an agent and I wondered why he had never told me to get one. And just at that moment, as if fate had planned it, I saw a photo of Brandon staring at me from the cover of a movie magazine on the rack. The cover was a collage of young faces with the headline "Stars of Tomorrow."

My whole next week I spent lining up several agents to see. My mother approved. The first agent I called was the number Top Pop had given me, and he said he could see me if I came around at two P.M. I cut school and tried to look extra special. I even took my portfolio, which was filled with pictures of myself in all sorts of artistic positions, leaping through the air, twirling, in dramatic agony, smiling as though for a toothpaste ad. I sat nervously in the agent's office, looking at the various posters hanging on the wall, posters of various shows and movies that his clients had obviously been in. I had picked up a copy of *People* magazine to keep me busy when the receptionist put down the telephone and said in an efficient voice, "Mr. Cole will see you now."

"Thank you," I smiled.

I walked into his office, which was filled with scripts and piles and piles of photos, obviously shots of people just like me, people who had pushed their way into his presence hoping he'd open up the world of show biz for them.

Mr. Cole, a well-dressed man about fifty, looked up and smiled.

"One second," he said, as he continued to read something that looked like a contract and then he looked up and smiled at me again.

"One second," he said again.

Then his phone rang.

"Pick up line two," the receptionist called in, and I was sitting there for over half an hour and he still hadn't talked to me. But finally it was my turn. "Do you have your resume?" he asked. I handed him a photo of myself with my credentials, height, weight, color of hair, plus my training and the little work I had done. I had included the time I had danced at the Brooklyn Veteran's Administration Hospital for sick G.I.'s.

"You're very pretty," he said. "Can you act?"

"Of course I can." I smiled confidently, not really knowing whether I could or not, although I had taken acting classes.

"That always helps," he said. "Can you dance?"

"Yes, I'm a great dancer," I said. "I've been dancing for eleven years."

I tried not to let my desperation show. Something
soon, not tomorrow, not next year, it had to be now,
now, I said to myself.

"Very well," Mr. Cole said. "If anything comes in
that you'll be right for, I'll call."

I was being dismissed again and I thought of my
mother and I burst into tears before I could get out of
the room. I stopped near the door, holding on to the
handle. "I'm sorry" was all I could say.

Mr. Cole cleared his throat. He didn't get up from
his desk. It was as though he was just observing me
with another big number on my back. But then he said,
"Miss Hillary, I think I know someone who would be
interested in you."

"You do?" I said, trying to stop crying.

"Yes," he said. "I'll tell him about you and have
him give you a call."

Without turning back, I said, "Thank you, thank
you very much, Mr. Cole." I walked quickly through
the receptionist's area, not wanting her to see me in
tears.

"Good-bye," I called over my shoulder and was
safely out into the hall, facing the gaping line of elevators.

When I got home that evening, it was the first
time my mother didn't have enough strength to come
to the dinner table. "Mom's much worse, isn't she?"
I asked my father.

"It doesn't look good, Brooke," he said.

"What can we do?" I asked him.

"All we can do," he said, "is try to keep her comfortable."

"But Dad," I started, "I hear her crying in the night and sometimes during the day now. The pain must be terrible."

"I give her a shot when the pain gets too bad." He came and sat down next to me at the dinner table and put his arm around me. "I know it's hard on you, Brooke."

"I'll do the dishes tonight, Dad," I said.

"No, honey, you just do your homework. I don't mind. It takes my mind off of my worries," Dad said. "The only real problem we're going to have now is to start lining up help to make sure that someone can be with Mom, so that I can still go to work and earn money; and you and Pete must keep going to school. Cousin Connie said she'd help out."

The phone rang.

"I'll get it," I said, jumping up from the table. There was an official voice at the other end. "I'd like to speak to Brooke Hillary," the voice said. For one wild moment I thought it was Brandon.

"Yes, this is Brooke," I said into the phone.

"This is Mr. Grant. Lou Cole called me and said you were a very beautiful girl and very talented."

"That was very nice of Mr. Cole. I hope I am," I said.

"Fine," Mr. Grant continued. "I'd like to line up an audition for you for Monday. Would you be available around eleven o'clock in the morning?"

"Oh, yes."

"I'm looking for a young actress to play in a new movie I'm doing. It's about a girl who's been captured by the Russians, a thriller."

"I like thrillers," I said.

"Then be at my office at eleven A.M." He gave me the address and I wrote it all down.

"Eleven sharp," Mr. Grant repeated.

"I got it," I said.

"And think *foreign intrigue*," he said.

I wrote down all the information as he was talking, my hand was shaking.

"Thank you so much, I said effusively. "Thank you so much for the interview, and I'm very thankful to Mr. Cole for submitting me."

"Don't mention it," he said. "Good luck." And then he hung up.

I turned to my father. "I have an audition on Monday for a movie! Isn't that something?" I said excitedly.

"That really is, Brooke," my father agreed.

"I can't wait to tell Mom."

"She'll be very happy," my father commented.

But as I ran upstairs to tell her, he called after me, "Just don't build up your hopes too much."

10

The next Monday at exactly ten-fifty-five I was sitting in a large impressive office waiting. There was no question, from the marble ashtrays to the chrome desk and plush red rug, that this was the big time. I knew I was at last meeting someone very powerful. Someone who would come through for me and my mother. I could still see my mother's eyes shining when I sat on her bed and told her the news. Her blood pressure had gotten very low and she had lost a lot of weight, but when I told her where I was going on Monday, she hugged me and we laughed and celebrated by eating half a box of Russell Stover candies.

"What time is it, please?" I asked the male receptionist. I had never been to an audition in an office that had a male receptionist before. He was very young and didn't look pleasant, though he was well dressed and had a fancy plaque on the front of his desk that said "Mr. Winters." "It's five minutes to eleven," the receptionist said.

"Oh yes, it is," I responded nervously. "I always try to be five minutes early for an appointment, then I know I'll be on time. Sometimes I even play tricks on myself by setting my watch ahead."

Mr. Winters seem unamused.

He annoyed me. I think the word I would use is that he worried me. Why, out of what must have been eight hundred auditions and interviews, had I never seen a male receptionist before? I busied myself looking around the room, reading a lot of the awards and film posters on the walls, and kept repeating to myself, *I'm not nervous. I'm relaxed. I'm as good as anyone else. I'm going to be fine.* But my exercises weren't working. I was nervous. I hoped it wouldn't show.

Then I decided I'd better go through this mental checklist which my mother had taught me to give me confidence at such moments: I was on time; I was neatly dressed; I had my photo and resume, and felt I looked pretty good.

I was still nervous. Then I resorted to repeating, *I'm a worthwhile human being, I'm special and I'm going to get the job this time.*

"Mr. Grant will see you," the receptionist interrupted. "This way, please." He stood up and showed me down a long hallway. He pointed to a door, and I opened it and went into a large office, the main furnishings of which were a desk, some sloppy chairs with a lot of pillows and a great many hanging plants. It had large heavy drapes instead of venetian blinds.

Mr. Grant got up and extended his hand. He looked like the kind of man who should be running a fish restaurant rather than producing a movie. He was short and heavy around the middle, and his chin tripled over as he looked down. He was probably around forty-five years old. He had kinky black hair combed straight back. There was something of a spry animal about him. His voice was deep and unhesitating. "It's nice to meet you, Brooke," he said, staring at me. "Please sit down," and he started reading my resume, which I had handed to him. He seemed to spend more time looking at me and my picture on the back than my credits, which was a good thing since my credits really weren't that good.

I kept telling myself that I wasn't shaking, but I really was and I didn't know where to put my hands. They felt funny swinging at my sides. I fidgeted with them and finally clasped them in front of me as though I was in church. For some reason I wanted to hide. I found myself pulling my skirt down, checking to make sure it had not crept up over my knee.

Mr. Grant's eyes were almost squinty as he peered at me.

"So you want to be an actress," he finally said, smiling broadly.

"Yes," I agreed.

"Well, it's a tough business, let me tell you that."

"I'm beginning to find that out," I agreed.

"How old are you?"

"Seventeen, going on eighteen," I lied.

"Really?" he said.

"No, not really," I said, lowering my head.

"Really I'm sixteen going on seventeen, but I can look older if you need it," I said.

"You're very pretty. You have a nice look. It's different." He seemed to have sensed my nervousness, which only made me more nervous.

"Relax," he said, "make yourself comfortable. I'm not going to bite."

I laughed and that did make me feel more comfortable, but it is a terrible job trying to look relaxed when you're really not. I watched him glance over my resume again. All the statistics of my life—my address and telephone number, what I had done, where I had studied. *Could he possibly be impressed? . . .* I thought.

"You haven't too much experience," Mr. Grant said.

"Well, I *am* only sixteen," I reminded him. "And I learn very fast," I said, with great energy.

"Well, you do have certain qualities that interest me," Mr. Grant stated. "But let's see if you can act." He passed me a very fancy, leather-bound copy of a movie script called *The Link Through the Berlin Corridor.* "Take a minute and look it over," he instructed. "You've got plenty of time."

I don't know if you've ever tried reading while someone else was watching you, but the words don't make any sense at all. I felt so self-conscious. He gave me almost no time before he spoke up. "Can you read a page or two?" he requested.

"Sure," I said confidently. But I didn't know how on earth I was going to get through it. *Just begin,* I told myself, *just begin.*

"Turn to page thirty-two," Mr. Grant instructed, as he opened his copy. "This girl, Laura," he continued, "has just come to the border of West Berlin and she is trying to reunite a small child with her mother and father. This is the scene where the guards are questioning you and this other little kid, but your job is to convince them that you're simply a tourist and you've got nothing to hide. Get it?" he asked.

"Right, I'm a simple tourist with nothing to hide," I repeated.

"Exactly," Mr. Grant urged.

I was surprised when Mr. Grant himself started reading the lines of the East Berlin guards, and as I read my lines, I could feel my nervousness fading. In fact, after the first few speeches, I'd say I was really getting into it, but after we had read two pages aloud, he looked up and said, "Very nice, Brooke."

He was nodding his head with definite approval and I began to think I stood a chance. In fact, I began to think I really stood a good chance, because Mr. Grant couldn't take his eyes off me.

"You really want this part?" he asked me.

"Desperately," I confessed.

He picked up on the word "desperately." "Yes," Mr. Grant said, "Mr. Cole told me you seemed to cry in his office about something. You have some sort of a problem?"

"Yes, Mr. Grant," I said.

"Would you mind telling me what it is?" he pursued.

He seemed very fatherly at the moment and I told

him. "My mother is very sick. She's dying and I would do anything to have even the slightest success before she died. I'll take anything, a walk-on, something without lines, anything no matter how small. But if I could go home and tell my mother that at least somebody wanted me for something, I can't tell you how happy it would make her. I can't tell you how much it would mean to me and my whole family. Anything, Mr. Grant, I'll do anything."

"What does she have?" Mr. Grant said without emotion.

"Cancer," I said.

"I see," he said, with about as much emotion as though I had told him she had a cold. I waited while he just stared at me. Finally, he continued, "Well, you see, Brooke, I might as well level with you. There are three other girls who are just as pretty as you and they gave good readings, too."

"Oh?" I said, and I could feel my chances slipping away. As usual, since there was competition, I was discouraged.

"Now, how do I pick one over the other, if they're all the same?" Mr. Grant asked, as though he was truly in a quandary.

"I don't know," I admitted sympathetically.

"You can call me Alan," he said and then continued, "I mean, Brooke, if each girl can do the part, then you realize that I have to pick the one who has something extra to offer, if you know what I mean." And by now he sounded very cold. "Business is business," he reinforced.

"I can understand that," I said.

"Specifically, Brooke, why should I pick you over the others unless you give me something, too?"

I was puzzled. I really didn't know what he was talking about, so I figured I'd better just ask. "What do you mean, Mr. Grant?"

"Look, you don't have to play simple," he said. "If you want to make it you're going to have to be very friendly with me, and if the director likes you and he wants you for the part, then you're going to have to be very friendly with him. That's the ballgame. And I'm talking about putting out, little girl."

I thought I must have misunderstood him. I couldn't believe this man wanted me to have sex with him, the director and God only knew who else for a part in a movie. Not that we hadn't made jokes at school about a "casting couch," but we really thought that was something that happened in the movies. And then the horrible thought came to me that this *was* it. I *was* in the movies and I felt sick to my stomach.

"I'm sorry, Mr. Grant," I said, getting up, and then I realized that I was still holding on to the script. I came forward to place the script on my chair. I didn't want to go near the desk.

"But you want to make your mother happy, don't you?" Mr. Grant inquired. "Your mother's dying," he reminded me, "and everyone has a price, you know. It's not even a price; it's called cooperation, and the sooner you learn that, the faster your career is going to move."

"I don't believe that," I said. "I believe one can

get ahead by working hard, not by your cheap way."

"Well, you better believe it, honey," he snapped.

"I guess you can say I have scruples. You missed out in that department!" I said.

"Right now, kid, you might as well know you may have scruples, but you don't have any talent. All you've got is a body. That's your only qualification for any job. And as far as I know, that's the only qualification you're ever going to have, because you're not exactly precocious in the emoting department, if you understand me."

"And you are not exactly a very nice person," I said.

"I never said I was," he said, returning to a more cajoling tone. "Brooke, I like you. I'll be very gentle with you. All you have to do is make your mother happy."

I turned and started back toward the door.

"Your mother's dying," he repeated.

I walked out. On the street the sun was blinding, but the wind blew and chilled me. I wanted to go home to my room and my mother and my father, and I wanted my brother, Pete. I wanted my own world where things like Mr. Grant didn't happen. I wanted my family and Nancy, and teachers and friends, all the hundreds of kind people who didn't take advantage. I wanted Brandon. I wanted to be a child again, playing in my closet. I wanted to bury my head in my mother's arms and have her rock me like a baby and tell me that everything was going to be all right, that the world wasn't the way it was beginning to seem. That there were still lovely things, a chance to be happy and to trust. I wanted my mother. I wanted her more than I had ever wanted her in my life. I wanted to hear from her that the world was not to be hated no matter what was happening to us. I wanted her comfort and all the warmth she gave me. I wanted to talk to her again, to the one person in the world no one would ever replace. I wanted to tell her about the ugliness that had happened to me and how I hurt, but I knew I couldn't do that. I had no right to do that anymore. Instead, I walked the streets the rest of the day, crying alone. And finally, when I couldn't cry anymore, I took the train back to Elmont.

"Hey, Ruby Lips," I heard an awful voice call out. "Hey, *you*—freaky Ruby Lips!" I began to cry again. I walked up the path to our house and I sat down on a bench behind a tree because I couldn't go in yet. I just sat there under my favorite big maple tree, the one that seemed to have grown with me, and I tried to gather myself together. And then, finally, I ran into the house. My mother was upstairs in bed.

"Is that you, Brooke?" she called, as I raced up the stairs. I flung open her door and, crying, kept repeating "Mom, oh, Mom." And then I just sat down on her bed sobbing, and she reached out and took me to her.

"Now, now," she said, comforting me. "It was only an audition, sweetheart. Don't cry, it's not the end of the world."

"Oh, it is, Mom, it is."

"This job wasn't meant to be."

"I just want to disappear," I said, and I pressed myself into her. Her body had become frail but was just as warm as it had ever been the millions of times I had come to her. Then it seemed as if she was reading my mind.

"Tell me what happened," she said. I knew she sensed something burning inside me.

"It's nothing," I lied.

"Brooke. Please don't tune me out. I might look a little fragile but I won't break. I need to feel involved. Please don't close me out. I don't want to feel alone."

"Mom, I'm not closing you out. Trust me." I got up and turned to the window.

"I hate to be dependent," she finally said.

"Oh, Mom," I said, turning back to her. A tear fell down her cheek. "Why don't I freshen you up?" I said. She nodded.

I washed her down with a warm cloth and changed her into her soft flannel nightgown. She asked me to brush her hair. Then I put some lemon cologne around her neck and I could see she felt more comfortable.

"How about some tea?" I asked.

"I'd like that." She smiled.

I went down to boil the water. When I came back she was glancing through a new book someone had brought as a gift. Most people knew by now that my mother was pretty much confined to bed. I set the tea down next to her bed and pulled a chair over to her side. Mom smiled, reassured that I would keep her company for a while. How long the day must seem just lying there by herself. I wondered what she thought about all those hours when she would stare up at the stucco ceiling. Was she preparing herself for dying? Was she frightened? Usually she was very practical.

"Brooke, I am going to set up two bank accounts at Federal National Bank, one in your name and one in Pete's. It's for you to do with as you wish. It's not much."

"Yes, Mom," I said. "Thank you." I didn't want to think of money.

"And the Boston fern in the living room has got to be watered once a week thoroughly, and sprayed every day."

"Yes, Mom. I know."

Other days, other cups of tea together—she told me to ask questions about things only she could really answer.

"What was I like as a little girl? Did I cry a lot?"

"Oh, no. Nothing threw you. And when you were very little you used to sing walking around with a blanket. You were a joy to have around," she said wistfully.

"And you. What were you and your mother like?"

"My mother was busy raising four kids and we didn't have all the conveniences you have now like freezers and processed food. Grandma used to get up early and start cooking. I always felt Grandma didn't have enough time for me."

"And Daddy. Did he ever go away for a while

when you were first in love—after he hit you with the bat?"

"Brooke," she said, laughing.

"Well, did he?"

"Your father was always a good man. A good boyfriend and a good husband. I was brought up thinking that my job was to get married. We liked being with each other, and we saw the world in the same way."

"Did you ever regret getting married?" I asked her.

My mother smiled. "Never," she said. "Sometimes I felt like being alone, but I think everyone wants a little privacy now and then, and when that feeling passed, I was very happy your father was there."

"But did you ever want more? Did you ever want more than this? More than Pete and me? More than this house?" I could tell she enjoyed being candid.

"Once I blamed Dad for my life being empty, while all the time I should have blamed myself. One day I just woke up and felt like a big zero. You and Pete were off at public school and involved with your own little lives. Dad was at work every day and I was at home being a big nothing. It was Dad who made me realize I had to find something. That's when I realized you could be a star for both of us. I wanted you to have more than what I had. Listen to me, talking to you like a confidante," she said, interrupting her train of thought.

"I'm flattered," I said. "Did you ever think of having another kid after Pete and me?" I asked.

"No—but once I had a miscarriage," she said matter-of-factly.

"I never knew that," I said incredulously.

"We never really talked about it before, Brooke."

"When?" I asked.

"A year after Pete was born I became pregnant and the doctor told me to take it easy. Around the fourth month I was mopping the floor and Dad told me to stop, that he would do it, but I insisted on finishing. When I was almost done, sharp pains shot through my abdomen and Dad rushed me to the hospital."

"What happened?" I asked.

"I lost the baby," she said sadly.

"How awful," I said, feeling her pain.

"Well, things work out for the best. A year and a half later I became pregnant again and it was you, Brooke," she said, philosophically content.

"Imagine losing a baby and having enough courage to have another. I couldn't do that," I said.

"Of course you could. The baby wasn't forming right and nature knows what it's doing."

"God," I said, "I'd be terrified to have a baby."

"Honey, when you're ready, it will be a very happy event," she said, brushing my hair away from my face. "And do you think those nine months are just for the baby?" she added. "No. Nature gives nine months' time for you too, in order to get ready mentally and emotionally to have the baby. Both you and the baby need time to prepare."

I just listened to her wide-eyed. "Weren't you scared?"

"I suppose for a few moments, but for me, looking back, giving birth was one of the most beautiful moments in my life. Dad and I made something very special together."

"You did?" I asked, wanting to hear more.

"We wanted a girl, and on the morning of May third you came out singing."

"You mean screaming." I laughed.

"Well, it might have been screaming, but it sounded like music to me."

"Mom. Then you really wanted me, didn't you? I wasn't an accident."

"Brooke, we wanted you more than anything. And we got you." We laughed together. "And you know something, Brooke," she added reflectively, "I could never have imagined living without you."

"Oh Mom," I said throwing my arms around her, "we are a team, aren't we?"

She smiled and nodded her head as she swallowed hard to hold back a flow of emotion breaking through like the evening tide. "You were such a dear baby," she managed to say.

"From the pictures I look funny-looking. Big ears. No hair. Something even a nursery might reject."

"Oh you were never funny-looking. Maybe for a few months, but when your hair came in and you became more a vertical person than horizontal, you were a doll."

"Oh Mom," I said, "no one can tell me those stories like you."

They were *our* stories and I wanted to store them all up, to know everything while there was still time, parts about me that would fill out the puzzle, parts that only my mother could know. After she was gone, all these memories, her thoughts, these were the things that she would leave behind on earth.

Suddenly the color had run from her face.

"Please, could you pull the blankets up? I feel cold," she asked. She hated feeling helpless! She watched me straighten the satin comforter and tuck it in close to her sides.

"I remember when I used to do this for you," she smiled. "Now I've become the baby. You're too young to have to take care of me. I'm so sorry."

I leaned over and kissed her forehead. "Mom, I love you," I said. "And I'm not too young."

11

Over a month went by and the two facts which re-
mained most clearly in my mind during that time were
Number One, that my mother didn't seem to get any
worse and Number Two, that I had not gotten any
more letters from Brandon.

Every day when I came home from school I would
run to the mailbox to see if there was a letter from him,
but there was none. *Brandon must be very engrossed in his
work,* I thought. The first magazine articles had come
out promoting him and the movie he was making, and
everyone at school was talking about it. Finally one
morning I woke up and knew I had to write to him. I
got a piece of paper and began to scrawl.

Dear Brandon, You have been in my thoughts lately so I
decided the best thing I could do would be just to write you
this letter. I realize that you are very occupied with your
career. I know you are already the *heartthrob* of practically
all the girls in the country, and Nancy and I love to see your
picture in the movie magazines. My career is going all right.

I've gotten myself an agent and I've been to a few auditions. I'm waiting to hear the results and a lot of them look very promising. I was offered one part that I didn't think was right for me, but I'm pretty sure the right role will come along. Wouldn't it be wonderful if we were both out in California at the same time?

I often look at the shell that you gave me on your secret island. I think of how the motor of the boat didn't start and we just drifted, not knowing if anyone would ever find us. You are terribly missed at school but no one misses you more than me. We're hoping that you'll be finished filming so you can make it to graduation at the end of May. That's not very far away.

My mother is feeling all right. She's been given some new experimental drugs and I hope she will get better. Please say hello to your mother for me and a special kiss to you. 1-4-3. Yours, Brooke.

I read the letter over and over and figured out that he'd probably receive it in about five days' time, and then I decided to read it one more time. I read all those lies about my career and I ripped the paper into shreds and got dressed to go to school.

In biology class that morning, Mrs. Phalan seemed to be reenacting the life cycle of gibbons and she got so involved in what she was doing, she made me forget we were in the Space Age. Nancy was sitting next to me and she passed me a note. I opened it. It said, "I hate war. Let's go to Switzerland. If not, let's meet right after class. I've got to tell you something."

I laughed at the note and smiled back at Nancy to tell her I was dying of curiosity to know what she had to say. Mrs. Phalan saw us exchanging glances and so we returned immediately to classroom protocol. That was one really nice thing about Mrs. Phalan, she never yelled at Nancy or me.

The phone rang in the classroom and Mrs. Phalan answered it. We all strained to listen, but she talked softly. All I could hear was "Okay, I'll tell her." When she hung up she said, "Brooke, the principal wants to see you after class."

"All right, Mrs. Phalan," I said. And then I thought, *God, what does she want to see me about? I hope my mother is all right.* For the entire rest of the class I couldn't concentrate, and Nancy looked at me reassuringly—she could see how worried I was. Finally, the bell rang and I jumped out of my seat. Nancy rushed with me over to the principal's office saying, "It's probably just about college plans or something."

"I hope so," I said as I opened the door, but all I kept worrying about was that something terrible had happened to my mother. Maybe she had been rushed to the hospital or something.

I had been in the principal's office only a few times over the two years. Once was just to deliver a note from my math teacher.

"Hello, Brooke. Dear, have a seat," she said.

"Thank you, Miss Hathaway," I said. Miss Hathaway had once been an officer in the Marines, but she was very statuesque and sophisticated and amazingly gentle.

"Don't look so worried," she said. "I have good news for you."

"You do?" I responded in amazement.

"Yes," she said. "We have selected you to represent our school on *The Tonight Show.*"

"I beg your pardon?" I interrupted.

"They're broadcasting from New York for a few weeks instead of Burbank and want to do a few minutes on talented children," Miss Hathaway explained. "They asked us to select one student we thought would represent us, and frankly, Brooke, most of the faculty decided you would be the perfect choice."

"Me?" I gulped in disbelief.

"Yes, you, Brooke. That dance you do to *Slaughter on Tenth Avenue* is really very, very good, and we think it's just right for television. They already have one kid who sings and another who does magic or something. But we think you're just what we need to make our school very proud."

"*The Tonight Show?*" I repeated. I couldn't believe what I was hearing. "I don't know what to say," I said.

"Don't worry about it. Just make sure you know what to dance," she said. "Put your best foot forward." She laughed.

"Oh, I will, Miss Hathaway. I will."

"Good. We'll be counting on you. Also, as part of the program, they want to interview a mother. They want to discuss what it's like to have a professional child, and I know your mother is the perfect choice. I remember her as president of the P.T.A. and she was a great speaker, very eloquent. And frankly, Brooke, I think the two of you will make a good package. We've dealt with the program before and they are a little stiff and structured, but I think your mother and you can make the best of it." The vision of my mother lying in bed crossed my mind.

"I'm sure she'll be thrilled," I said. "Thank you. Thank you very much."

I left the office in a daze. I couldn't believe it. My mother and I had been selected over all the others, and I knew it wasn't a sympathy vote because neither Miss Hathaway nor any of the other teachers knew how sick my mother was.

"What is it?" Nancy asked, jumping up and down in the hallway, looking apprehensive.

"Miss Hathaway just selected me to be on a television show. *The Tonight Show.* She picked me to represent the school," I said.

"That's terrific, Brooke." Nancy was genuinely happy! "Congratulations."

"And my mother," I continued, "they want to interview her, too. Imagine that. They want to ask her what it's like to have a kid in show business."

Nancy looked confused—her excitement seemed mixed with another emotion. "Do you think your mother will be able to make it?" she asked.

I said, "For something like this, of course she'll be able to make it." But deep down I wasn't quite sure. I wasn't sure at all.

Nancy said, "I'm so happy for you."

We walked down the stairs toward French class.

"Nancy," I asked, "what was it you wanted to tell *me*?"

"Oh, it's not important."

"Yes, tell me."

"No. Some other time."

"That's not fair," I said. "You can't say you have something to say and then change your mind," I said. "Say it."

"Well, it's just that my mother and father told me this morning we're moving to Colorado!"

"When?"

"Next week."

"It's impossible."

"No, it isn't. My father has been transferred there and my mother says some of the best ice-skating coaches work out of there."

I realized why Nancy had dreaded telling me, because she knew that I could never tell her that I would be leaving her. She was my best friend. We told each other everything. The hours we'd spent planning our lives, making major decisions on whom we would marry, the houses we wanted, the trips to Europe we'd take. All the schemes and plans we'd worked on about how to get Brandon to notice me, and the boys she'd had crushes on to ask her out. And now she was moving away and taking our friendship and dreams with her. It was like separating the white from the milk: It can't be done.

"If only they'd picked you to be on the television show," I said. "Maybe then your father would see how you had to stay here for your career," I reasoned out.

"I'm sure they wouldn't throw an ice ring on *The Tonight Show*," Nancy said, laughing.

"Maybe they would," I said, hugging her. "Nancy," I said seriously, "how can I come to school each day without you here? How can we take another test if we don't study together? Get nervous together? Get sick together? Remember how our stomachs growled at the same time before a history exam? We're sisters. You can't separate sisters."

"Let's tell my father that, Brooke. You know when he makes up his mind to do something."

"Well, tell him you don't want to move and you don't want to be stretched anymore!" I ordered.

"But it makes my father so happy!" Nancy laughed.

"There should be a law against children being relocated and stretched!" My attempt at humor didn't ease the pain.

"Brooke, I don't want to go and I've tried everything, but it's no use."

I knew Nancy had had nothing to do with the decision, but it didn't make my being hurt any less real. And again I began to feel resentment that someone I really cared about was leaving me. There was a major theme forming in my life—anyone I loved too much I lost. Nancy was leaving for Colorado, Brandon was in California, and even Pete. And my mother most of all! Patterns. My life seemed to be following a pattern that anything I cared about was taken away. There was no permanence in anything. Things were changing too fast for me, and I didn't know how to hold together the pieces falling away. I felt alone.

Nancy sensed this as she took my hand and smiled. "Brooke, I love you. You'll always be my best friend. Always." And I looked up and felt tears forming in my eyes. Our friendship made me feel warm and good and alive.

"Nancy, are you really sure you want to be an ice skater?"

"I try not to think about it. One time I told my father that I wanted to be an astrophysicist and he cried for two weeks and mumbled, 'All those years of study, all that money down the drain.'"

I looked at her sympathetically because I knew her father was very good at making her feel guilty. "Why don't you stay at my house until school is over?"

"Listen. I've been through it all with my folks. I've done the crying. Ranting. Raving. My father insists I go out there with him, and you know something, Brooke, I hate to admit it but I think I love ice-skating. Sometimes I like ice-skating because it lets me get away from him. He can't keep up with me on ice. But I've come to the conclusion that if you do something long enough, you get good at it. And I've got to face it, the best ice-skating coaches *are* in Colorado. And I'll tell you something else—I do want to make it more than anything."

"You will. I know you will," I said. "But what will I do without you here? And our phone bills! How much does it cost to call Colorado?"

"Come out and visit me."

"I think I really should give a party for you."

"No. I don't even want five people at Rudley's for ice-cream sodas. I want to disappear quietly," Nancy said.

"You sound frightened."

"No. I've learned there's no room for fright in this business. I'm learning to be cold-blooded in every sense of the word. Besides, Colorado won't be so bad with all the good-looking ski instructors around. Anyway, I've got it all planned—you come out in August and we'll take a raft down the Colorado River. We'll hitchhike to Mexico and do something absolutely crazy!"

My feeling of desertion was back.

I remembered on the boat Brandon took my hand and promised me I wouldn't be alone. Well he was wrong. And when I confessed to him I was afraid that everything I cared about would die, he put his arm around me and told me not to be afraid. Well, where was he now? I needed his arm around me *now*. Maybe I needed a course more practical than history, or mythology—maybe I needed a class in survival. I could see how Marilyn Monroe had finally felt too much pain. She could have used a course like that too. One thing I was sure of, I didn't want to be alone. I spent the rest of the school day daydreaming about my mother's reaction to the news that we'd both be on TV together. When school was over I ran to catch a 2:20 train home.

The train pulled into the station and I was back in Elmont. I tried to forget for a moment about Nancy leaving, and Brandon leaving, and Pete leaving, and my mother's sickness, and thought about sharing the news about *The Tonight Show* with my mother. I practically jumped over the hedges and flew into the house. "Mom, Mom," I yelled. I ran up the stairs, taking two steps at a time. My mother was sitting up in bed reading. "Mom, the school picked me to be on television. I'm going to be on *The Tonight Show*. From the whole school, they picked me! Can you imagine? I can't believe it."

My mother's eyes lit up with a combination of excitement and curiosity. "You're kidding," she said.

"No, I'm not kidding. It's real, it's *true*. This time it's the real thing."

"Oh, my God," my mother said. "Isn't that something? My little girl's going to be on television."

"I'm going to represent the school."

"Oh, Brooke, I'm so proud of you." And then she gave me a great big hug. "I knew it was just a matter of time."

"And guess what else," I said, practically exploding.

"What?" she asked.

"They want you to be on the show, too."

"Me?" She looked shocked. "What for?"

"They want to interview you. Ask you a few questions about what it's like to have a brat in show business and all that. How do you like that?" And I laughed even more.

"You're joking," my mother said.

"No, I'm not. Miss Hathaway told me herself."

For a moment, my mother looked very serious. "What did you say when she suggested that?"

"Nothing," I said. "I told her you'd be thrilled. Miss Hathaway said she'd selected you because you were such a good speaker. So eloquent, that's what she said. Exactly those words. She said you were eloquent."

"But, Brooke, that was *before*," my mother started slowly. "Look at me. I can hardly walk. How can I get up and speak on a show, a television show? How can I be in front of television cameras? How can I do it?" she asked.

"Of course you can," I insisted. "You can rest up for the whole week and then Dad can drive us in. You won't have to do much. You sit there, like you sit here in your chair, and you'll answer some questions and you'll be yourself."

"I don't know, Brooke," Mom said. "I just don't know if I could do it." But this time I could see a twinkle weaving its way out of her eyes. I saw her eyes begin to sparkle. I could tell she loved the idea.

"Okay, Brooke, I'll give it a try," she said, and I could see the old fighting spirit going back into her. "I've always known you would be a star," she said, as she gave me a big kiss. "And I'd make it, too!"

"I'm so happy," I told her. "I'm so happy. You're sure that it won't be too much for you?" I asked, only after she had consented to do it.

"I can't think of a better way to get exhausted." My mother beamed. "This is what we've been working for your whole life."

I couldn't wait to write Brandon the news. I felt so wonderful scribbling away, and I tried not to sound like I was bragging—I just wrote him the good news, except for the part where I told him I was losing Nancy. I didn't rip up that letter.

The show was scheduled for March 15th, and for the next few weeks I came home from school after my dancing classes, with the exception of a "good-bye" hamburger with Nancy at Rumpelmayer's soda fountain, which was a sad and tearful farewell. Somehow we got through it, even invented a date in August for my visit. And then Nancy was gone.

I practiced my routine over and over and over. I stopped going on auditions and open calls—I just wanted to practice and concentrate on doing my best. Everyone was counting on me. Everyone would be watching, my mother, my father, Miss Hathaway, Pete at school. I didn't want to let any of them down. I wanted to be everything my mother knew a Hillary could be!

On March 11th I came home from school and my mother was sitting up in bed and adding several rows of sequins to the already oversequined outfit. "Do you think you'll be ready in time?" she asked anxiously. "Are you timing everything so that it will be perfect for the show?"

"I think so," I said. I'm never overconfident, but somehow I did feel confidence this time. This time, it seemed that truth was going to be stranger than fiction, stranger than any symphony that was ever written, stranger than anything I had ever seen in the world of art. I felt as though this had been planned for my mother, to make certain she felt she hadn't lived in vain.

"Are you ready," I asked her, "to knock them on their ears?"

"You bet," she said.

"You have it easy," I said gently. "All you have to do is be yourself and you'll be terrific. You always do a great job at being honest." But then her face contorted in sudden pain. "What's the matter?" I asked her.

"This isn't one of my better days," she said.

"Can I do anything for you?" I said, putting my arm around her.

She tried to smile. "I hate to ask you," she said, "but would you mind giving me a shot of Demerol?"

"Okay."

"You sure you don't mind? I'd try to do it myself, but I've been having trouble turning."

"No, I don't mind," I said lightly, so as not to embarrass her. I went and filled up the syringe in the bathroom and I came back out, took a deep breath and gave my mother the shot. For someone who hated getting a shot like myself, it wasn't easy for me to do. I know I have no talent when it comes to giving injections. I was concerned, too, because my father had told me that Demerol was a narcotic and that it was the strongest painkiller that existed other than morphine and heroin.

"Can I do anything else for you?" I inquired.

"Just sit here with me awhile," my mother said, as she lay back on the bed and closed her eyes to rest. She took my hand in hers and I sat quietly next to her as she drifted off to sleep. I covered her with the rose-colored comforter and watched her for a while. I wasn't going to let anything hurt her and I wasn't going to let her down. I knew that in the last few months she had been teaching me another lesson, whether she had wanted to or not. And that was the lesson in how to be brave and human and proud. I wanted more than ever to succeed for my mother because I knew how important it was for her. It was more important that I succeed for her than for myself. And I think she was only lasting as long as she was because she needed to be with me for one last triumph, one moment of glory together.

I was worried about my mother's being able to make it. Every time she asked me if I thought she would be able to do it, I always told her, "Definitely, yes." But deep down, I really wasn't sure. Finally, the day came for the television show. We were told to be at the studio by five o'clock. I didn't go to school because Miss Hathaway told me I could take the day off and rest up for the evening. Late afternoon I took out my mother's clothes and laid out her makeup.

"I'm feeling fine," she said.

"Have you taken your medication?" I wanted to know.

"Yes, I did. And I've got a couple of pills. They should hold me over. I don't want to sound like a drunk on television," she said.

"You could never sound that way," I told her, but I prayed she could do it the way she wanted to. I didn't care about myself, but now I cared more than ever about her. Oddly, what most excited her was that an old friend of hers, a lady who had moved out to Oregon and who had been her friend for many years, would be watching her. My mother had called her. She had called everybody. I guess everybody in the family had called everyone we knew on earth and said, "Watch the Hillarys. Watch the Hillarys on March fifteenth."

"I have your costume in the tote bag, and your tape," my mother said.

"Thank you, Mom."

"Your father made some tuna salad. I thought you should eat a little before we go."

"I'm not hungry," I said.

"You must be very nervous, honey."

"A little bit," I admitted.

"That's to be expected," she said.

Just then, the front doorbell rang and a boy was delivering a long white box tied with a bright red bow and unmistakably containing flowers. The box felt smooth and cool, and I carried it into the house. It was the first time anyone had ever sent me flowers. The outside card read "For Claire and Brooke Hillary." Who could have sent us flowers? I thought. I wanted to tear open the box.

"Mom. Mom. Flowers came for us," I said, rushing up to her room, the box almost flying out of my arms.

"Open it," she said, giving me the honors.

"Who could have sent us flowers?" I asked with excitement as I carefully undid the ribbon and put it aside to save and opened the box. Inside, lying on a pillow of soft pink tissue paper, were the deepest red-velvet roses I have ever seen. "Aren't they beautiful?"

I said as I pulled the flowers to my nose and the sweet smell reminded me of the very expensive perfume Joy that my cousin Connie used to wear and would sometimes put a dab of behind my ear. My mother opened the card.

"Who sent it? Who sent it?" I said, dying of curiosity, thinking it might be from Brandon.

"It's from Pete," my mother said jubilantly. " 'For my little sister,' " she said, reading every word carefully, " 'and my great mom. Good luck. Love, Pete.' " My mother's face lit up and I don't think she could have gotten a more beautiful present.

I felt thrilled that my brother had sent us flowers, and I hoped Brandon might think of doing it, too. Sending flowers was a lovely idea and I hoped it would happen again. "I'll get a vase," I said.

"Get the big crystal one in the dining room," my mother requested. That was the finest one in the house, reserved for special occasions. I picked each rose up and handed it to her as she carefully arranged them. I put the box and ribbon in my closet to save, maybe to keep old cards and pictures.

When my father came home he was taken aback by the unexpected bouquet of flowers my brother had sent. He only had time to gobble down a tuna fish sandwich and a glass of juice before we had to get into the car.

"Don't worry. We'll just beat the rush hour," he said.

I ran up to my room to get my tote bag and saw my mother placing an envelope on my brother's dresser. It seemed odd she would write a note to my brother when he was at school, but she always said to write a note at the moment you were filled with the emotion. And besides, Pete was expected home any weekend now. She then picked up her bag and went downstairs.

"Hurry, Brooke," she called after me, "we'll be late."

"Coming," I yelled down, but my curiosity about the envelope compelled me to go into Pete's room. Quietly, I walked in and picked it up. It wasn't sealed. Now, one rule in this house was we never opened anyone else's mail. We respected each other's privacy. But I had a burning curiosity to know in what private way my mother and brother spoke to each other. Did she speak to Pete differently than she spoke to me? I opened it, knowing it was wrong for me to do so. The note was neatly written in my mother's handwriting on her fine stationery.

Dear Pete, Thank you so much for your most thoughtful gift. I was both thrilled and proud of you. It was not the idea of the gift but the feeling and consideration it showed. Your display of fine character makes me proud you are my son. Love, Mom.

My mother's voice coming from the kitchen caught me in my transgression and I felt guilty. "Brooke, hurry!" she yelled up.

I thought my heart would stop, I got so scared thinking I could be caught in my sneaky act. Carefully, I placed the letter back in the envelope and ran out of the room. I knew that my mother and Pete did indeed share something very special.

My father began to sing in the car as we raced along the Long Island Expressway. My mother was wrapped up in her coat and I held her hand. She kept smiling and fidgeting and she was very excited. We all seemed so happy, and yet I was afraid something terrible was going to happen. I was afraid the car would crash or that the bridge would break, that some unknown, unforeseeable obstacle would come hurtling into the way and crush us. But the trip was uneventful and we arrived at the television studio in time. Then things started moving very quickly.

A makeup man took me and my mother into a room and started slapping powder all over our faces, just like they do with all the famous television personalities. We looked very different, but the makeup people told us we would look just like ourselves when we went out over the airwaves. My mother was doing beautifully; no one would ever have known she was ill, and she deserved an award for the way she had been holding up so far. She was doing it for me and I was doing it for her and yet, above it all, I felt that she was being driven by a force stronger than herself.

Then a man came over. "Ten minutes," he shouted at us. I was to dance, then my mother would be interviewed. As usual, the adrenaline started pouring through my body and I started doing my warmup exercises.

"Five minutes," the stage manager called to me.

My mother was being pulled away to another part of the backstage area. She blew me a kiss and we wished each other luck. "You'll be great," I told her. She came back to me and took my hand—or I took hers—but somehow we were holding on to each other for dear life.

"I forgot my dance, Mom," I called out. "How does it start?"

"At three beats you run and then do a row of turns into a walkover," my mother said calmly.

"But what if I fall?" I complained.

"You *won't* fall," she reassured me. And now she was out of sight.

My fear wouldn't stop. I kept thinking I wouldn't make it, maybe I'd fall on my face in front of the television cameras.

"Places, please," the stage manager said.

Then I heard the announcer say, ". . . and here's Brooke Hillary doing a modern dance rendition of *Slaughter on Tenth Avenue.*" Suddenly the lights were on me, the director standing behind the cameraman gave me the cue and it was my moment. The music started to play. All I thought about was the sound of the music, and somehow the dance came back to me automatically, as though I wasn't remembering it at all, as though my body was moving by itself. Then it was over. I had finished. I was on the floor in the right position and people in the television studio were applauding loudly. I didn't know whether I was coming or going until I heard my mother's voice from a TV monitor and I realized she was being interviewed. She was asked, "How does it feel to have a child studying theater?"

"Well, it's very exciting." My mother spoke softly. "Because at a young age my daughter has direction and discipline and knows what she wants. This is something people who are fifty years old sometimes are still searching for."

"Do you think she can live a normal life and still pursue a life in the theater?" she was asked.

"Of course she can," my mother said with conviction, though her voice was very weak. "She's getting a good education in school and she has a normal homelife with me and her father, who love her very much, as well as her brother Pete, who's very proud of her as well." I was glad she mentioned Pete, too. "And," she continued, "we make it a point to teach her that she can do anything she wants to in life, if she works hard for it. But she must never, never sacrifice her own self-esteem and dignity for anything. Her name is the most important thing she's got. And she must always be proud of it, whatever it is she decides to do in life. In this case, Brooke wants to have a life in the theater, and if that's what she wants, we support her wholeheartedly."

"Well, I think you should be very proud of your daughter, and I know that the future will hold a lot of exciting things for you both. And I thank you, Mrs. Hillary, for talking with us this evening."

"And thank you for asking me," she said. "It's

been a great privilege." Then I watched as my mother managed to get up and walk off with great dignity. She smiled graciously, hiding the enormous anguish and pain she must have been feeling just having to sit in one position under the hot lights. No one would ever have known that she was going to die. In her way, she had choreographed her own dance and she had given the performance of her life. I ran over to her. "Oh, Mom, you were wonderful."

"We did it. We did it, didn't we?" she said triumphantly.

"We make a great team," I said.

My father put his arm around Mom to help her; he was very happy and he told us all the glowing things people were saying in the audience. And then we saw the principal and a few other teachers I hadn't even known were in the audience. They congratulated us on how well we represented the school. And then as we drove home—my father, my mother and I—we talked at a feverish pace about every nuance of the evening. We went over each and every point and how well it had gone, and we sang together. It seemed like we had never been happier before in our lives. By the time we arrived my mother wanted to go back to bed. She asked me to help her get out of her dress and into a lavender-and-green nightgown that was freshly washed.

"The way you made your entrance. It was electric," my mother said.

We had a hard time getting her arm out of the dress. It was causing her a great deal of pain. My mother continued, "I could see you were enjoying it. Your face was aglow."

It looked like the day had taken every ounce of energy from her as I eased her into bed. She leaned on me as I helped her swing her legs under the comforter. I puffed up her pillows. She grasped my hands for support as she lowered herself backward.

When she sank back on the pillows she was trembling. "This is going to lead to your big break."

"Mom, do you need a shot?" I asked, seeing she was not going to admit she was in pain.

"Thank you," my mother said. "Yes, I think so." And as I got the needle and bottle of Demerol my mother said, "Even the cameramen thought you were sensational." She said it I guess to take her mind off the pain.

I prepared the injection and held the needle. My mother pointed to a spot on her skin. I did the best I could as she talked swiftly about the future and what my next dance should be. I knew she wanted me to think I wasn't hurting her. The only thing that gave me strength to give her the shot was that I knew in a few minutes it would take her out of her pain. Her hand clasped mine.

"Sit with me a few minutes," she said. She closed her eyes and waited. Then she opened them and spoke in a small, weak and terrified voice. "You've got to get a good agent. It's important to strike while the iron's hot. Lots of people saw you on the show and will remember you—but they won't remember you forever."

*Is this woman withering away in front of me my mother?
The person who has always been vibrant and strong, who had
the energy of four teenagers wrapped up in one, is this thin
person now my mother?* I looked at this skinny lady and
said it was impossible for her to have changed that
much. Her face had thinned down, which changed the
shape; her eyes had lost the glisten that used to light
up any room. And her arms had thinned down to a
child's size. I remembered her carrying thousands of
bags of groceries into the kitchen through the years,
saying, "There's a few goodies in here you'll be interested in." She'd always wanted to lose fifteen pounds
and she'd talked about it for years, but I never minded
her slight roundness—it was kind of nice and soft,
especially when I would curl up in the back of the car
and fall asleep on her lap when my father was driving.
Now looking at her it was hard to imagine that she was
once my age and having crushes. It was hard to imagine that I was once a seed growing inside her, that she
had nurtured me as she carried me around in her
womb for nine months, taking me every place with
her, then with her own force had pushed me out, all
seven pounds of me, and made me a separate human
being.

I suppose I thought about that because right now
my mother's energy was directed at holding on to her
own life and there was no way that I could sustain her
life as she had sustained mine. She worked hard on
eating but had no appetite; she tried to walk but her
bones couldn't support her. If the world had some

grand design, why didn't it invent a more merciful way of leaving this earth? I could hardly recognize her, and I wanted to cry out, *I want my mother back the way she was.* But this wasn't a game we were playing, and I couldn't take my dolls and go home.

Instead I saw her hand resting by her side and I picked her hand up and pulled it close to me. Her fingers seemed very skinny to my touch, and as I pulled her hand in toward me, her wedding band came flying off and fell to the floor.

"Ohh. Get that for me!" my mother said urgently.

"Okay, Mom," I said reassuringly, trying to hide my surprise at how hard she had worked all these weeks to keep it on.

"Here it is," I said as I held it up. It was a single gold ring with my parents' initials and the date they were married. She had worn it twenty-four years without taking it off. That's a long time.

"Give it to me," she said.

"It's so big. Why don't I put it in the drawer next to your bed?" I asked.

"No," she said forcefully. "This I won't take off. I'd feel naked without it," she insisted.

"All right," I said, handing it to her.

"I want always to wear this ring. Always. Do you understand, Brooke?" she said as she put the ring back on the finger.

"Yes, Mom. I understand."

"Always," she whispered. And I knew she meant even after death. It was impossible for me to understand how my mother could accept the fact that soon she would have to give up everything in this world— her marriage, Pete, me, all she cared about, her hopes and her vision of me becoming the star she had always wanted to be, and even the gentle sounds of the summer to come.

12

Nancy and I wrote to each other a great deal during April, all about her new school and the mountains of Colorado—but I still didn't hear from Brandon. I had sent three notes to him at different hotels and one to his home in New York hoping his family would forward it to wherever he was. I dreamed he saw me on the TV show and wrote me a letter telling me how proud he was of me and that he thought I danced beautifully and that he still loved me. Some days I would leave school and go directly to the magazine stand on Fifty-seventh Street to see if the fan magazines had any new photos or column items about him. I would pore through the racks wishing so hard he could be with me that I hurt. Sometimes I would talk silently with God and ask Him for just one more day with him and then I wouldn't ask for anything more the rest of my life. I was beginning to go out of my mind with pain and fear. I loved Brandon so much that the front of my mind felt as though it was being paralyzed and the wall holding up my sanity was about to break. Finally, I couldn't stand it anymore and I wrote him the truth. I not only didn't play games, I decided to beg him. "Dear Brandon," I wrote,

I love you so much I think of you day and night and I feel like I'm going to die. I don't want to embarrass you but I need your help desperately. I do nothing but think of kissing you and holding you and being with you. You haven't written in so long! I know you are working hard, but if you have any feelings for me you've got to let me know. I'll do anything for you. If you want me to fly out there I will. I'll stay with you at your hotel or anywhere. Please write. Please, Brandon. I beg you, I beg you. I love you. I love you. Forgive me for loving you, Brooke.

I mailed this letter.

Finally a letter arrived, and I tore open the envelope.

Dear Brooke, I saw you and your mother on television and you were terrific. It made me want to come rushing home, but that doesn't seem likely. My agent just called telling me that I got another movie, which should begin shooting in about two weeks. So my mother said it's really not worth coming back to New York for such a short period of time. It seems like I won't be there for graduation. They'll be sending me my diploma. I always figured the tassels on those hats would tickle me anyway.

I've been getting so many offers that now we spend a lot of evenings reading possible movie scripts. My agent says I have to be very careful about what I accept, because a wrong picture could stop my career. They even arranged for a limousine to take me to the studio every morning.

Yesterday I was having lunch at the Beverly Hills Hotel

with my agent when a group of girls came over and asked me for my autograph and a kiss. People are really beginning to recognize me on the street. I forgot to tell you, it looks like I might be going to France next month. On top of that, my father is going to buy me a Corvette for my seventeenth birthday. Cars are really important out here, because we spend so much time in them, and I think I'll really look good in a Corvette. Keep up the image. I've been invited to a lot of parties. When we first arrived in Hollywood, we went to a lot of B and C parties, but now we are invited to some A parties. Those are the best ones, with lots of movie stars and people of my caliber. Two things I learned out here was that they like you when you are working and the more money you have the more they respect you.

I'll try to send you a postcard from France, and give my love to all the kids at school. See ya. Brandon.

I put the letter down. He hadn't signed 1-4-3. He hadn't signed much of anything. In fact, from his letter I realized it didn't matter very much whether he had received my last cry for help before writing it or not. I didn't even want to read it over. I couldn't believe it.

This was not the same boy who had left New York just a short time ago, the gentle, sensitive person whom I was willing to devote my whole life to, the one whom I loved with all that was in me. How could he change so much? The letter was shallow. It was less than shallow. Does this happen when you go to Hollywood? Does all that glitter and all that adulation from others make you into a callous person who could forget friends? Could the memory of what we shared that day on the beach, all those private talks, end like a movie? Capture it on celluloid, then put it in the can. From the letter, Brandon seemed like a stranger to me. I didn't like him anymore, not if he could forget those he cared about, not if he could change his values like a chameleon. Then I made a promise to myself: If I ever made it, I would never forget my family, my friends, or where I came from. Because that was what meant the most to me!

I was in my room when I made that promise and I suddenly became aware of voices coming from my mother's room. I knew it was my mother and father talking, but then I was aware of the fact that the talking had stopped and now there was only crying. I moved to the door of my room and listened.

"Put me out of my torture. Look at me! I've just become a body. I'm tired of being experimented on! Just let me go, Jack! Let me go! What's the use anymore?"

I sank down onto the floor of my room. Never had I felt more tormented. I wanted to shut out the sounds of my mother begging to die in the next room as I sat there helplessly on the floor. I whispered, *"Mom, I know the pain must be terrible, but don't leave us all. Please don't leave yet."*

I heard my father say, "As long as you're alive, there's hope."

My mother cried, "There's no hope, there's no hope anymore."

I put my face down onto the rug and tears flowed. I was crying for her and my father and myself and for Brandon, too. My mother began to cry for help. Her voice became a whisper. A violent whisper, "Help me, help me." What would I do if she asked me to leave the bottle of pills next to her pillow when I was alone with her? How would I answer her pain?

After a few more minutes, my mother stopped crying and they stopped talking. I heard my father coming out of the room. I moved away from my door so he couldn't see me, and I heard my father go into the bathroom for a tissue to blow his nose. I felt sorry for him, for everybody. My mother hadn't been out of bed since *The Tonight Show*. She had moved into a combination of Demerol and morphine, which left her drowsy almost all of the time. Sometimes she was incoherent. Some mornings she would try to put her makeup on and then burst into tears.

Finally, it was May and my graduation would be in a week. All the kids got only four tickets, which would have been enough for me. The only people I wanted at my graduation were my mother, my father and Pete, so I would have even had an extra ticket. I thought of Brandon and tried not to cry. I wished Nancy would be there but that was impossible. The exercises were going to be held at Carnegie Hall in the morning. And even though I knew my mother couldn't go, I took the tickets and left them next to my mother's bed while she was sleeping. I felt it would bring her joy to know that I was officially graduating, even though she wouldn't be able to come to the ceremonies. I never talked about the upcoming graduation to her. I knew she wouldn't be able to go, and any discussion of it would only make it harder. I felt I would just get dressed that morning and probably my father would go. My brother might drive down from college to stay home with my mother and that would be it.

The morning of graduation day I got up, washed my face and stumbled right into my mother's room to help her over her disappointment. Instead, I was surprised to see her sitting on the edge of her bed. She asked me to help her get her blue jersey dress over her head. She already had her makeup on. She looked very sick, but she stood up and began to walk slowly. I could hardly believe my eyes. She hadn't been able to get out of bed for so long, and here she was walking by herself.

"Are you getting ready?" she said to me as if this was an everyday sight.

"Mom, you're walking!" I said, astonished.

"Of course I'm walking," she said, proud of herself.

I watched in amazement as she moved around her room.

"Come here a minute," she said. "We have something for you, Dad and I." She handed me a present.

"What is it?" I asked. And she just watched me untie the blue bow and open the small box. Inside it was a velvet case containing a ring with a familiar pearl in the center surrounded by twelve diamond chips forming a heart.

"You remember the pearl from my ring?" my mother said. "I had it put into the center of yours," she said. "Do you like it? *The pearl is yours now.*"

"It's beautiful," I said, as I slipped it on my finger. "It's very, very beautiful." And then I kissed her.

"Wear it well," my mother said, smiling. And I put my hand over the ring and held it as if it were a delicate bird that might fly away. I couldn't believe it! The ring that I had always loved was now mine! A part of my grandmother, a part of my mother, had now been passed on to me, and I suddenly felt like I was growing up. I remember my mother telling me the ring represented "Freedom." And in that moment I was overtaken with the awesome sense of power I had and the connection I served between the past and the future. "Freedom"—the word poured out jubilantly without any hestitation, and my mother just smiled.

The pearl felt warm as I pulled it in toward me, as if I was holding my mother close to me, and I knew this moment would last forever.

"Thank you," I whispered as I threw my arms around her and gave her another kiss.

We went to the graduation, all of us, Mom, Dad, Pete, who had come home, and me. My mother sat there proudly as they played "Pomp and Circumstance," and she watched me walk up and receive my diploma. She never took her eyes off me for a second and I never took my eyes off her, because as incomprehensible as it seemed, I knew that in a matter of time I would only be able to see her with my eyes closed.

13

A few weeks had gone by since the graduation, and my mother's condition had worsened. She would lapse from consciousness to unconsciousness all day and night. And one time when I was with her alone she said, "Brooke, how are things going?" And I knew she was still thinking about my career.

"Fine," I said, smiling and trying to give her hope even though I was lying.

"Good," she said, then drifted back to sleep.

Once she asked me for her makeup case and she used her lipstick instead of her eyebrow pencil to darken her eyebrows. I took a tissue and wiped it off.

I sat next to her on the cold special hospital-type bed we had rented for her. It had a crank and an air mattress. I would sit with her for hours, and even when she was awake, sometimes we'd just stare at each other or she'd say a word and I'd know she'd know I was there.

One morning in particular I heard my father outside cutting the lawn. I went to the window and threw it open, letting in that watermelon aroma of freshly cut grass, then picked up the scent of lilacs which grew around the trellis under my mother's window. I took a long deep breath.

"Can you smell them, Mom? The lilacs are in bloom."

Her eyes were closed and it seemed like she was drifting into one of those deep sleeps she was getting more frequently, yet her mouth broke into a big smile. I don't know exactly where she was, but I knew she heard me. Knowing that it made her happy, I went down and cut some fresh lilacs and placed them next to her bed so she could smell them in her sleep.

Not long after that came the day when my mother opened her mouth and said, "Well, I guess I've had it." She gave me a smile of defeat. I reached over to embrace her, but her body wasn't able to respond much anymore. "I just want to drink you all in while there's still time," she said as she held on to me.

"I'll always be here for you," I said, caressing her gently.

Then I couldn't talk. I wished I could tell her how good it was to just feel her hand in mine. That simple pleasure meant so much!

"What are you thinking about? You're smiling," I said.

"I'm seeing my life in Technicolor. I see my mother playing with me in the park when I was five. My eighth-grade yearbook. *Oh, Claire, Full of grace. Everyone loves a pretty face.* My best friend, Eva. Dad and me at

Brighton Beach. You. Pete. The summers in the mountains together."

I listened as the tears ran down my face. All those memories flying before her eyes. Is this what happens before you die? Was that it? Was my mother's life passing before her? Was this what dying was? I sat next to her watching her sleep. How vulnerable she looked.

Then I heard her say something.

"What did you say?" I asked.

"I want to die here. Not in a hospital. I want to die at home," she whispered.

"Okay, Mom," I said.

She opened her eyes. "I don't want to make you unhappy anymore," she said.

"Mom, you've never made me unhappy," I cried. "You've given me everything I could have ever wanted. I would do anything in the world for you," I said.

"That might have been a problem, Brooke," she said. Words seemed to flow out of her now as though there was no holding them back. There wasn't time to hold back now.

"Maybe I was too selfish," she said. "I'm not trying to make excuses, Brooke. I know I wasn't a perfect mother. I don't think I could have been."

"Mom, you couldn't have been a better mother to me."

"Forgive me for anything I might have done to hurt you."

"You didn't hurt me, Mom. Please don't say that."

She closed her eyes and I felt for her pulse. I could feel her heart was still fighting. I sat back and looked at what my mother had become. She had been so vibrant, laughing and making people laugh with her. Now she was a ghost. She weighed less than seventy pounds, just a shell of what she once had been—and it broke my heart.

In two days it would be Saturday, the twenty-fifth of June. That was her birthday. She would be forty-six, too young to die. There was hardly a discussion about what to do to celebrate the day, because my mother wasn't aware what day it would be, but *we* would know, the rest of the family. We thought we could at least have a cake, and even though she didn't need it I had bought her a new nightgown with rosebuds and a satin ribbon so she could change into it on her birthday.

Saturday morning arrived and my mother appeared to be feeling better than she had in weeks. It seemed like she was giving *us* a present. She was able to eat a little bit of applesauce and I had cut some red roses from the garden. Before noon I went to the main shopping street in Elmont to pick up the birthday cake. I bought some candles and my mother's favorite ice cream. When I arrived back home an ambulance was in front of the house. *It's happening,* I thought as I ran up the steps. Two large men in white uniforms were putting my mother on a stretcher. My Aunt Faye and Cousin Connie were there talking to my father.

"What's happening?!" I cried out. "What's happening?!" My father pulled me to him and put his arm around my shoulder as the men carried my mother out.

"Is she gone?" I asked in fear.

"She's unconscious. The doctors say it's almost over."

"But you can't take her away. You can't take her to the hospital. I promised her she would spend her last moments at home, not in a hospital!"

"They may be able to help her die easier."

"But she'll be all alone. This is her home. She can't be alone. Not now." I began to cry.

"She doesn't know that anymore, honey. She's going from us," he said and looked down with total resignation.

The men were wheeling her through the door. "It's her birthday today," I told the men, but they just looked at me and continued with their job.

"Brooke," my father said, "I'll go with Mom. You wait for Pete. He's driving back down. It shouldn't take him more than a few hours and then I'll see you both at the hospital." He got into the ambulance with my mother. The others followed behind in their car.

I stood on the front steps of the house. This time it was me waving good-bye to my mother as she had done to me since I was a little girl. As I shut the door, the emptiness closed around me. I walked through the kitchen, the living room, the dining room, almost re-tracing every step my mother ever took, trying to fill the empty house. Then I ran upstairs into her room and threw myself onto her bed. I held her pillow and hugged it and buried my face in it. All I knew was that

I wanted to be close to her, and I became hysterical as I took her blanket, the blanket that had touched her body for all those years, and covered myself with it. I tucked myself in it and I rolled in it and I cried and I hid under it and I caressed it. I felt insane, I felt alone and abandoned and I wanted my mother back. I saw everything in her room, her flannel bathrobe, the picture of us smiling together at the studio right after the television show, her Bible. I just wanted to hug everything, to be close to everything she had touched. I rolled back and forth on the bed and I cried out, "Mom, Mom, you're still here. You haven't left! All your things are still warm! This is your home! You'll be back and we'll continue to be a great team! You and me! We'll knock them dead at the next audition! Remember Lassie liked me! Remember everyone loved you!" *Remember how we laughed when the blue skirt came off my costume unexpectedly and I turned my routine into a bullfighting dance? Remember when we walked down the street and went shopping together? I was always proud of you because you had a vision for me and you gave it to me. I'm going to make it, Ma. You've got to be here to see it. What is the good of my getting it if you can't be there to share it with me? This will always be your room, Mom, and I will always be your little girl. Things will never change, Mom, don't worry about that. Come home, Mom, come home.*

I must have lain there for hours and then finally the phone rang. It was my father's voice.

"Mom's dead, Brooke," he said, gently. "I'm sorry, honey. I'm very sorry." And then for the first time in my life, I heard my father crying.

14

Pete and I met my father at the funeral home to make final arrangements and to select a coffin for our mother. The salesman-undertaker showed us around quoting the best features of each model and the costs. My father asked just a few questions and then selected a bronze casket that was not too ostentatious.

Just one last thing," my father said to the funeral director. "My wife wants her casket closed. Claire said she wanted people to remember her as she was before her sickness."

"Of course." The director nodded, and we started out of the room. I couldn't wait to leave that place of lifeless smells and phony formality where funeral directors spend their entire lives playing sad. Ours was a terrible actor. He reminded us before leaving that we should bring Mom's clothes over to the funeral home before five o'clock so that she could be dressed before seven, even though she wouldn't be seen. It was still customary, he told us, even though the lid would be shut—and friends and relatives would be coming to pay their respects from seven to ten P.M. After their private good-byes, the funeral would take place the next morning: Sunday, a day of rest.

My father made some phone calls when we arrived home, but I could see it was a great strain on him so I told him I would call the rest of the people. I also called in an obituary to the local paper. It was simple and straightforward, just the facts. Then my father asked me to select a dress and whatever other clothes would be needed for my mother. I knew he couldn't do that part himself.

I went up the stairs and turned toward my mother's room—but I couldn't go in. Instead, I went into my own room and closed the door. I climbed onto my bed and lay there motionless, absolutely unable to move. I felt dead like my mother, and noticed I was lying there as stiff and lifeless as if I was in a coffin, too. I felt unbearably lost, totally alone. *I lived to make you happy,* I found myself thinking in a message to my mother. *You were my hope and now you have left me.* I lay there quietly but my thoughts flooded my mind. I was confused because I was starting to feel things other than love and a sense of loss. I began to feel a sense of my own mortality, that one day I too would die. I felt as though I was suffocating, and a feeling of bitterness toward my mother began to emerge, swelling inside me. I was exploding inside. I thought of screaming out for help. It was as though I was spitting up years of feelings which had been bottled up inside me. My eyes darted to the telephone, but then moved past it to my closet door. I got up off my bed slowly and moved toward it. Somehow I found myself standing in my closet, and it seemed as if the voices of my childhood began to rush at me from everything my eyes beheld. A thousand different voices. My mother's voice, strong, instructing, *Jump higher, Brooke. Go for greater elevation! Brooke, now you have to remember that you're going to be a very great star. Brooke, this dress is too plain for you. You need pizzazz. No one is going to look at a plain Jane. Paint your lips. Eyelashes, you'll need eyelashes to make your eyes so big they'll be seen from the last row of the balcony!* "But Mom," I'd say, "I don't want people to always look at me." And she would say, *You're a born extrovert.*

As I looked at a decade of clothes I heard my childish voice pleading, "Mom, which shoes do you like?" *The blue,* she'd say. *They make you look at least two feet taller.* Ghosts were flying at me from the shoe racks, from the rows and rows of costumes, from old toys, teddy bears and carousels and even an old crib. Strange hats my mother thought I should wear. Dusty shelves filled with memories of silver dollars I had won from her in Scrabble games. My old third-grade report card she had refused to sign because the teacher gave me a C in something. *She's an A student,* my mother had yelled into the telephone. *An A!* A little girl's voice was saying, "No, Mom, please. That embarrasses me. Please, Mom, don't." And there were photo albums Mom and I had put together all those nights trying to preserve our family history. *You're going to be the greatest star coming out of the Hillary family, even if it kills me!* "But

Mom, Mom, please—I don't want to take another dance class. I want to go play with my friends. I want to go roller-skating. I want to play softball." *Well, Brooke, you mustn't waste your time. Anyway, you could break your ankle.* The sight of the costumes now was like seeing monsters jumping out at me—all the times I had to perform and be judged and rejected.

I found my original birth certificate with my baby footprint on it so I wouldn't be mixed up in the hospital nursery. There was a gold locket my parents had given me when I graduated from sixth grade, but it was crushed. And my dolls. They were all lined up, staring at me. My favorite was Erica. She wasn't very beautiful anymore but she was still soft and reliable. I remembered how I used to gather all my dolls at night and could never go to sleep unless they were lying down, too, with their eyes shut so I knew they were comfortable. The games we played were in a special corner, the games the whole family played. Chinese checkers. Clue. Games for when I was sick in bed. Games to make me happy. Games we'd play when there was a power failure and only candlelight to spin the spinner or draw a card by. I found a picture of myself when I was four. I looked innocent and rather sweet I thought, but my mother had touched up the picture. Put longer eyelashes on with a pencil. *Why did you do that, Mom? Why did you make me look like a freak? No little kid has eyelashes like that!* It was at that moment I saw clearly that whoever it was who had walked into this closet years ago—whoever that little girl was—had died. My childhood, my youth, my own voice which had once been loud and clear, had slowly been murdered in my closet. It had all been lost when my mother had convinced herself that I should become a dancer. It seemed ironic to me that the closet—where I had always gone to hide, to share my deepest feelings, my most precious secrets of self—had been so totally invaded. I remembered it had been the only place I could stand naked. I could never undress in my room itself. I'd always run into the closet, where I thought I would be able to escape—but I couldn't.

I came out and shut the closet door. I went to my vanity table and switched on the bright lights that framed the mirror. I couldn't help remembering all the times I had been spinning at a ballet class in front of a wall mirror, catching reflections of myself, sometimes my mother—never being quite sure where my mother began and I ended. I took out a jar of special moisturizing cream by Elizabeth Arden that my mother had given me with instructions—*You must take care of your face if you want to look young even when you're my age!* I looked at my face carefully and I looked into my eyes. I had a great deal of makeup on, the makeup my mother wanted me to wear. I moved my face closer, closer until I felt as though I was seeing myself for the first time in many years. I felt as though I was in a movie house, that I was looking at Marilyn Monroe with her face covered, her eyes crying out, "Help me. Help save me." And I heard someone calling. Deep in my head a horrible voice was calling, "Hey, Ruby Lips! Hey, Ruby Lips!" I smeared the cream all over my face and scrubbed the layers of makeup off with a tissue. I took some baby oil and rubbed off all the mascara on my eyes. I wiped my lips until they were clean, and I brushed my hair away from my face to get rid of the Snow White bangs that my mother thought were a good attention getter and helped compensate for the shape of my brow. I wiped my lips until they burned, until I was certain there wasn't a shade of anything that didn't belong naturally to Brooke Hillary. Finally, I sat back and looked. What I saw was a simple, unadorned young girl. A teenage girl. Someone not too bad.

I wanted to hate my mother. I sat there trying to hate everything she had done to me, for I really felt it had been horrible. But something inside of me wouldn't let me feel hate. My mother was too good. She was too good, no matter how neurotic she had made me—no matter how hard she had tried to make me into another person. She couldn't have loved me so much, held me all those years, without having seen beyond herself to leave me a legacy to save myself— some secret to make me come alive again. Open some door.

I glanced down to the ring on my finger—the ring with the pearl in the center she had given me for graduation. The pearl that had been passed from my grandmother to my mother and now to me! *Freedom!* And as I touched the pearl I decided it had to stand for all the best parts of my mother. I remembered her qualities of bravery, her enthusiasm, her aliveness and her enormous ability to love—which she had passed on to me. Then I noticed the set of diamonds which whirled around the pearl forming a heart, an orbit of its own. My mother had said: *People look for Mars and Jupiter in the skies, but inside of us is where we find our own dreams.* I remembered her saying that over and over, pointing to her heart. *You must believe in yourself, but you must feel it in here!* Contradictions, I thought. Why so many contradictions? If she forced me to look for the truth about myself, why did she want to create such an artificial image of who I should be? It seemed inconsistent. My Mom was a good mother, but there must have been some part of her that was unfulfilled and she couldn't help trying to find it in me. But I decided no matter what, she did want the best for me, too. It just came out all wrong. Maybe that's why she gave me the ability to fight and the ability to be a very strong person, so that I could fight for what I wanted just like my mother had fought for what she wanted.

At that moment I looked at myself in the mirror and said my first truthful words in years. "I don't want to dance," I said aloud, and it was as though a curse had been broken. A great relief came over me and I could feel the blood of Life beginning to flow inside of me again. And I realized that approval wasn't what I wanted anymore, and became filled with a need to please myself. It was getting late and there were things to be done.

I went into my mother's bedroom and picked the blue jersey dress she had worn on the television show because I knew it was the happiest moment my mother and I had shared together. Then I went to pick out shoes, but I knew she really wouldn't need any. It was then I realized there was something in my room I would have to get. Something of my own I would have to take to the funeral parlor for Mom and myself. I put her stuff over my arm, went back to my room and pulled out my pink toe slippers—my dance shoes with the long satin ribbons. I washed my face clean, I put on a dark dress—the only black dress my mother had let me buy—and to cover my hair I wore a black chiffon scarf. I put my mother's clothes into a shopping bag and slipped my dancing shoes into my own purse. I went downstairs and gave my father the shopping bag. "Here it is," I said.

We went to the funeral parlor—Pete, my father and I—and my father gave the clothes to the funeral director. He told us to come back at six-thirty, which would give us a few minutes alone with Mom before the guests started to arrive. We drove to a delicatessen and ate sandwiches and didn't say too much. When we arrived at the funeral home I walked directly into the parlor where my mother's coffin was placed, surrounded by flowers. My father started to say a prayer but started crying when the pain got too intense and had to leave the room and sit down in the foyer. "Pete," I said softly, "why don't you take Dad to the men's room. Washing his face and having you with him might help before all the people arrive and the next ordeal starts." Pete nodded and took my father downstairs. I was now alone in the room with the casket except for the funeral director, who was placing a basket of yellow roses next to the casket. I moved quickly to him.

"Please open the casket," I said. "I want to see my mother," and I was surprised by the sound of the force in my own voice.

He looked surprised but then managed to regain his smooth formality. "I wouldn't advise that. Her hair isn't done and she isn't wearing makeup . . ."

"Open it," I cut him off. He undid a couple of latches muttering, "It's supposed to be a closed coffin. . . ."

"I have a right to say good-bye to my mother," I said.

My mother looked more peaceful than she had for months. All the pain she had been holding in was now released from her face. There was a great serenity, a calm. I pulled my dance shoes from my bag, wrapped the ribbons gently around them and placed the shoes in the coffin next to her. I told the funeral director to close the coffin, which he did without asking any questions. He left the room and I spoke silently to my mother. *I may not be what you want me to be, but I do hope, whatever I choose, that you'll be proud of me. I love you, even though you influenced me too strongly and we've been too closely linked to each other. You were doing the best you could to be a good mother. There was so much you did give me—the joy and zest for life and being able to love—and forgive.*

And Mom, there's something else I've got to tell you. You told me that I have choices in life, and for the first time in my life I know what you mean. I feel free.

There were voices. I turned around and some of my friends had just arrived. There were Rosalyn and Joy and Leslie from the mythology class. I went to greet them and they said how sorry they were. Then my Aunt Faye and Uncle Mike came in, and by this time my father and Pete had come back and started receiving all my mother's friends and relatives. There were so many people who cared about her. Remembered her. Pete came over to me and took me aside.

"You all right?" he asked.

"Yes," I said.

He looked at me carefully as though he had noticed the change. "Brooke, you've never looked more beautiful," Pete said.

What a strange remark for him to make at this moment, I thought. What an inappropriate time—but then I could see in his eyes that what had been my discovery that afternoon was something he had known all along. He understood more than I did. I nodded to him, but then saw my father standing at the doorway looking like he needed some support. How much I loved my father, I thought. I hardly knew him, it seemed—he had been so shadowed by my mother and I wanted to know more about him. He looked like he needed me, so I went to him, not because my mother would have wanted me to but because I wanted to myself. I stood by him.

It was funny. This was the end in one way, but it was the beginning in another. And there was one thing I was sure of. I realized that the only star I had to be was the one that glows inside me, the star that only I could be, the star of my own dreams. I'm a little late in starting, many other kids my age already know more about themselves than I do—but for me this is a beginning.

FONTANA · LIONS

Compelling reading from Fontana Lions for older readers:

- ☐ **Wounded Knee** Dee Brown **90p**
- ☐ **Grimm Grange** William Browning **85p**
- ☐ **The Chocolate War** Robert Cormier **95p**
- ☐ **I Am The Cheese** Robert Cormier **95p**
- ☐ **Come to Mecca** Farrukh Dhondy **60p**
- ☐ **Red Shift** Alan Garner **90p**
- ☐ **The Outsiders** S. E. Hinton **80p**
- ☐ **No End To Yesterday** Shelagh Macdonald **95p**
- ☐ **My Mate Shofiq** Jan Needle **70p**
- ☐ **Z For Zachariah** Robert O'Brien **90p**
- ☐ **Into the Road** Adrienne Richard **75p**
- ☐ **The Sword in the Stone** T. H. White **95p**
- ☐ **My Darling My Hamburger** Paul Zindel **90p**
- ☐ **Confessions of a Teenage Baboon** Paul Zindel **70p**

Fontana Lions are available in bookshops, and can also be ordered by post.

HOW TO ORDER

FONTANA LIONS BOOKS, Cash Sales Dept., GPO Box 29, Douglas, Isle of Man, British Isles. Please send purchase price of book plus **Postage**, as follows:—

    1–4 Books.........10p per copy

    5 Books or more ......no further charge

    25 Books sent post free within U.K.

Overseas Customers

    12 per copy.

NAME (Block letters) _____

ADDRESS _____

_____

_____